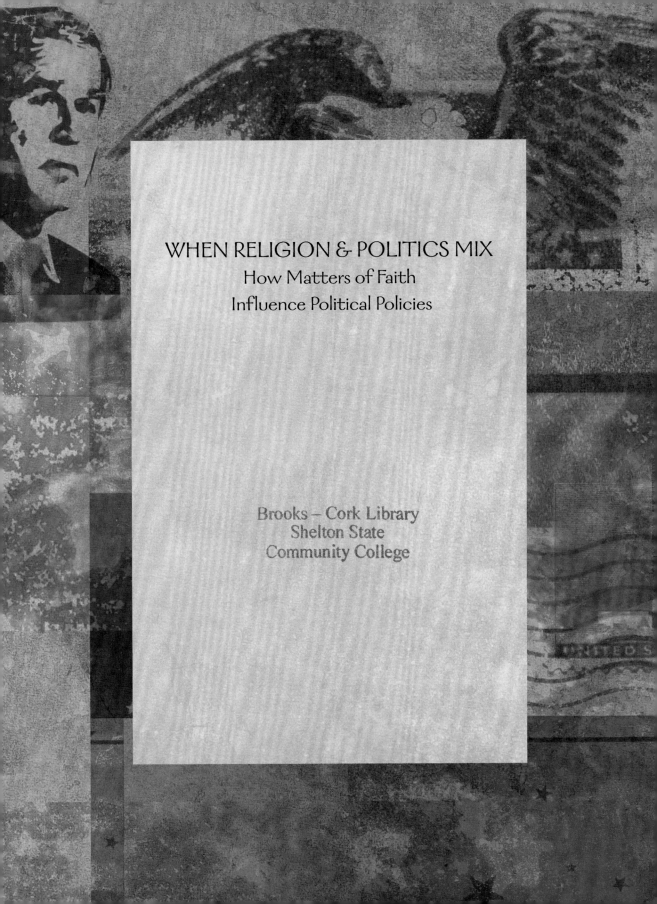

# WHEN RELIGION & POLITICS MIX
## How Matters of Faith
## Influence Political Policies

# RELIGION & MODERN CULTURE
## Title List

# WHEN RELIGION & POLITICS MIX
## How Matters of Faith
## Influence Political Policies

by Kenneth McIntosh, M.Div.,
and Marsha McIntosh

Mason Crest Publishers
Philadelphia

Mason Crest Publishers Inc.
370 Reed Road
Broomall, Pennsylvania 19008
(866) MCP-BOOK (toll free)

First printing
1 2 3 4 5 6 7 8 9 10

Library of Congress Cataloging-in-Publication Data

McIntosh, Kenneth, 1959–
   When religion and politics mix : how matters of faith influence political poli-
cies / by Kenneth McIntosh and Marsha McIntosh.
      p. cm. — (Religion and modern culture)
   Includes index.
   ISBN 1-59084-971-X   ISBN 1-59087-970-1 (series)
   1. Church and state—United States—Juvenile literature. 2. Church and social
problems—United States—Juvenile literature. 3. Religion and politics—United
States—Juvenile literature. I. McIntosh, Marsha. II. Title. III. Series.
   BR115.P7M353 2005
   201'.72'0973—dc22

                           2005003057

Produced by Harding House Publishing Service, Inc.
www.hardinghousepages.com
Interior design by Dianne Hodack.
Cover design by MK Bassett-Harvey.
Printed in India.

# CONTENTS

# INTRODUCTION

by Dr. Marcus J. Borg

You are about to begin an important and exciting experience: the study of modern religion. Knowing about religion—and religions—is vital for understanding our neighbors, whether they live down the street or across the globe.

Despite the modern trend toward religious doubt, most of the world's population continues to be religious. Of the approximately six billion people alive today, around two billion are Christians, one billion are Muslims, 800 million are Hindus, and 400 million are Buddhists. Smaller numbers are Sikhs, Shinto, Confucian, Taoist, Jewish, and indigenous religions.

Religion plays an especially important role in North America. The United States is the most religious country in the Western world: about 80 percent of Americans say that religion is "important" or "very important" to them. Around 95 percent say they believe in God. These figures are very different in Europe, where the percentages are much smaller. Canada is "in between": the figures are lower than for the United States, but significantly higher than in Europe. In Canada, 68 percent of citizens say religion is of "high importance," and 81 percent believe in God or a higher being.

The United States is largely Christian. Around 80 percent describe themselves as Christian. In Canada, professing Christians are 77 percent of the population. But religious diversity is growing. According to Harvard scholar Diana Eck's recent book *A New Religious America*, the United States has recently become the most religiously diverse country in the world. Canada is also a country of great religious variety.

Fifty years ago, religious diversity in the United States meant Protestants, Catholics, and Jews, but since the 1960s, immigration from Asia, the Middle East, and Africa has dramatically increased the number of people practicing other religions. There are now about six million Muslims, four million Buddhists, and a million Hindus in the United States. To compare these figures to two historically important Protestant denominations in the United States, about 3.5 million are Presbyterians and 2.5 million are Episcopalians. There are more Buddhists in the United States than either of these denominations, and as many Muslims as the two denominations combined. This means that knowing about other religions is not just knowing about people in other parts of the world—but about knowing people in our schools, workplaces, and neighborhoods.

Moreover, religious diversity does not simply exist between religions. It is found within Christianity itself:

• There are many different forms of Christian worship. They range from Quaker silence to contemporary worship with rock music to traditional liturgical worship among Catholics and Episcopalians to Pentecostal enthusiasm and speaking in tongues.

- Christians are divided about the importance of an afterlife. For some, the next life—a paradise beyond death—is their primary motive for being Christian. For other Christians, the afterlife does not matter nearly as much. Instead, a relationship with God that transforms our lives this side of death is the primary motive.
- Christians are divided about the Bible. Some are biblical literalists who believe that the Bible is to be interpreted literally and factually as the inerrant revelation of God, true in every respect and true for all time. Other Christians understand the Bible more symbolically as the witness of two ancient communities—biblical Israel and early Christianity—to their life with God.

Christians are also divided about the role of religion in public life. Some understand "separation of church and state" to mean "separation of religion and politics." Other Christians seek to bring Christian values into public life. Some (commonly called "the Christian Right") are concerned with public policy issues such as abortion, prayer in schools, marriage as only heterosexual, and pornography. Still other Christians name the central public policy issues as American imperialism, war, economic injustice, racism, health care, and so forth. For the first group, values are primarily concerned with individual behavior. For the second group, values are also concerned with group behavior and social systems. The study of religion in North America involves not only becoming aware of other religions but also becoming aware of differences within Christianity itself. Such study can help us to understand people with different convictions and practices.

And there is one more reason why such study is important and exciting: religions deal with the largest questions of life. These questions are intellectual, moral, and personal. Most centrally, they are:

- What is real? The religions of the world agree that "the real" is more than the space-time world of matter and energy.
- How then shall we live?
- How can we be "in touch" with "the real"? How can we connect with it and become more deeply centered in it?

This series will put you in touch with other ways of seeing reality and how to live.

# Chapter 1

# DIVIDED YET INSEPARABLE:
## Politics & Religion
## in North America

RELIGION & MODERN CULTURE

It is early morning in Washington, D.C. Over the White House, jet fighters patrol the skies. Businesspersons and politicians are just waking up, getting their morning coffee, reading the newspaper, and preparing for the day.

Have you ever wondered, *What is the president of the United States doing at this hour? How does he start his day?* Every morning, even before his first cup of coffee, George W. Bush spends a few minutes alone praying and reading a book of **devotional** thoughts. Like millions of other Americans, the president says that devotion to God is an important part of his life.

Although not all Americans practice the same variety of spirituality as President Bush, many Americans would agree that religion is a vital aspect of their national identity. Some of the earliest European settlers came to America for religious reasons, and religion has played a role in the shape of American government and politics, right from the very beginning.

## THE FIRST AMENDMENT

In 1791, the Founding Fathers added the Bill of Rights, the first ten amendments, to the U.S. Constitution. The First Amendment guarantees religious liberty. It begins, "Congress shall make no law respecting establishment of religion, or prohibiting the free exercise thereof." This means that the U.S. government cannot create a national church or officially support one religion over another. The second half of the First Amendment means that the government cannot prevent people from practicing their religion.

Some people say the First Amendment is a wall between politics and religion that keeps the two completely separate. Others see the First Amendment more like a fence between neighbors. It separates politics and religion but leaves room for plenty of conversation between the two.

Religious and political experts have struggled to apply the First Amendment appropriately to specific issues. For example, the Pledge of Allegiance says we serve "one nation, under God." Does that mean the government supports *monotheism*—and does the pledge refer to one specific religion's concept of God? At times the government has tried to stop religious believers from worshipping in ways that could harm their health—such as handling deadly snakes or taking mind-altering drugs. Does that violate freedom of religion? The separation of church and state seems like a simple idea, but it's not always easy to apply in real life.

# GLOSSARY

**agnostic**: Someone who believes that the existence or nonexistence of God is impossible to know.

**atheist**: Someone who does not believe in God.

**Christian Peacemaker Team**: A group comprised of Christian volunteers who work for justice and peacemaking where there are violent conflicts in the world.

**conservative**: Traditional, unwilling to accept change.

**demographics**: Characteristics of a human population.

**denomination**: A smaller grouping within a larger religious body or faith.

**devotional**: Expressing or relating to religious feeling, prayer, or worship.

**divisive**: Causing disagreement or hostility within a group so that it is likely to split.

**evangelical**: Relating to a Protestant church that believes in the authority of the Bible and salvation through the personal acceptance of Jesus Christ as savior.

**liberal**: Open-minded, willing to accept change, not bound by authoritarianism.

**monotheism**: The belief that there is only one God.

**Protestants**: Members of a Christian church who do not see themselves as connected to the Roman Catholic heritage and who reject Catholic authority.

**secular**: Not concerned with or controlled by religious or spiritual matters.

**theology**: The study of religion.

**Vatican**: The Catholic pope's headquarters in Rome.

**Western**: Countries whose culture and society are greatly influenced by traditions rooted in Greek and Roman culture and in Christianity.

RELIGION & MODERN CULTURE

*"Religion plays a much larger role in U.S. elections and government policies than most people think."*

—*Kathlyn Gay*, Church and State

## POLITICS & FAITH IN THE UNITED STATES

A popular expression states that "politics and faith don't mix." Yet they do; inevitably, the two concepts influence each other. As Kathlyn Gay points out in her book *Church and State*, "from America's earliest days, religious leaders and groups have taken stands on many political issues." Furthermore, she asserts, "religion plays a much larger role in U.S. elections and government policies than most people think." One reason for religion's influence in politics is that America has a representative government. Through voting, citizens choose leaders to represent their opinions and needs. For many people in the United States, religion is a key factor in how they vote.

A recent study by the Pew Forum on Religion & Public Life concluded, "The United States stands virtually alone among the world's wealthiest nations in the value its people place on religion in both their private lives and the public square." According to Luis Lugo, director of the Pew Forum, 75 percent of Americans approve of President Bush stating he relies on his religious beliefs to make decisions. Half of Americans say they would not vote for an **atheist**. Nearly 60 percent believe journalists should question politicians regarding their religious beliefs. And religion's influence doesn't end with influencing how citizens will vote. Once a leader is elected to office, that individual's personal religious views can play a significant role in the formulation and approval of official government policy.

Religion's influence in American politics can be **divisive**. The United States is increasingly diverse in terms of religion, and differing religious beliefs can land voters and elected officials on either side of

*13*

controversial issues. One person's beliefs may lead her to support an issue, while another person's beliefs may lead him to reject the same issue. Consider the most controversial issues in American politics and society today: war in Iraq, stem-cell research, gay marriage, and abortion. Many citizens and elected officials take stands on these issues based on their religious beliefs. In some ways, this is nothing new—religion has always played a significant role in American political life. Religion's influence is particularly visible in today's American White House.

## FAITH IN THE WHITE HOUSE

According to British writer G. K. Chesterton, America is "a nation with the soul of a church," in which each president serves as pastor. *Newsweek* chief political correspondent Howard Fineman claims, "Every president invokes God and asks his blessing." He goes on to note that, "This president [referring to George W. Bush]—this presidency—is the most resolutely 'faith based' in modern times."

The Bush family has always been church-going **Protestants**. President George W. Bush, however, has been especially committed to his Christian faith. This was not always the case, however.

"W" grew up with many advantages. His father was a wealthy owner of oil businesses in Texas with powerful political connections. In 1977, George W. Bush married, and in 1981, he and his wife, Laura, had twin daughters. However, Bush was a heavy partier, and his drinking troubled his wife. That changed in 1985 when Bush joined a Bible study group. Influenced by biblical teachings, George W. Bush made a public claim to stop drinking alcohol.

Since becoming president, Bush has repeatedly quoted from the Bible in important national speeches. Shortly before the Iraq war, he told a national prayer breakfast, "Behind all of life and all of history

## GOD OR CAESAR?

The struggle between church and state is by no means new. In the Gospels of the Christian Bible, accounts of Jesus's life, religious authorities ask Jesus, "Should we pay taxes to Caesar?" At the time, the Roman armies occupied the Jewish nation, and many people resented paying taxes to their conquerors. Jesus requested a coin and asked, "Whose image is on this coin?" The people replied, "Caesar." Jesus then said, "Give to Caesar what belongs to Caesar, and give to God what belongs to God." The book of Genesis says human beings were made "in God's image," which has led some Bible scholars to interpret Jesus's words as meaning humans owe God allegiance in everything, while they owe their earthly leader only limited obedience. How much religion and politics should influence each other is a question people continue to struggle with today.

there is a dedication and a purpose, set by the hand of a just and faithful God."

Insiders say there is much talk of God in the White House. Former attorney general John Ashcroft says President Bush commands America's armed forces but "understands that it is faith and prayer that

*"Though it is very important for man as an individual that his religion should be true, that is not the case for society."*

—*Alexis de Tocqueville*

are the sources of this nation's strength." The president's chief political adviser, Karl Rove, has worked very deliberately with George W. Bush to gain the trust and votes of *evangelical* Christians. Michael Gerson, the president's main speechwriter, studied *theology* in college and attends Bible studies with the president. Chief of Staff Andrew Card is married to a Methodist minister. National Security Adviser Condoleeza Rice is a preacher's daughter.

Not everyone, however, is thrilled with the president's outspoken faith. Critics—including Christian ones—are concerned that the president sometimes confuses "God's opinion" with his own. In June 2003, a group of 120 leaders from President Bush's *denomination*, the United Methodist Church, signed a magazine ad asking him to "repent" of what they claim are policies "incompatible" with Christian faith. They protested his policies regarding the environment, war, and the needs of the poor. According to a *Worldnet* report, the White House responded: "The president respects the views of those placing the ad but does not agree with them." In a similar show of disagreement with the role the president's faith plays in his decision making, the Sojourners, a Christian group in Washington, D.C., gained thousands of signatures and raised significant support to run a campaign before the 2004 presidential election. They proclaimed in the media and on bumper stickers that "God is not a Republican—or a Democrat."

Some critics also feel that the current administration's particular type of religious focus may be creating an atmosphere that leads to intolerance of other religious groups, something that many Christians say is a direct contradiction of basic Christian principles. For example, in early 2004, reports emerged that U.S. troops tortured Iraqi prisoners at

17

Baghdad's Abu Ghraib prison. Many religious leaders and organizations responded with criticism of the president and administration. Although President Bush decried the actions at Abu Ghraib, some political and religious critics blamed his administration for their occurrence. Basic administrative policies had apparently led to regarding torture as an acceptable way to treat prisoners. Furthermore, the prisoners were Muslim, and to many people the abuses appeared to be not only torture of the individual prisoners but also degradation and disrespect for the entire Muslim world. Many questioned whether President Bush, his administration, and even the U.S. population as a whole, influenced as they are by certain religious views, could fully comprehend the impact these actions would have on the Muslim world.

Christian groups and leaders were some of the ones who spoke out most strongly against the events at Abu Ghraib. According to several news sources, a **Christian Peacemaker Team** presented the first report of the prison abuses to leaders of the coalition forces in Iraq. Religious groups around the world condemned the treatment of Iraqi prisoners. The National Council of Churches called for U.S. forces in Iraq to turn authority over to the United Nations. A **Vatican** official said photographs of prisoner abuse were "a more serious blow to the United States than September 11."

While some Christians are critical of George W. Bush's policies and performance, many others support him. In the 2004 election, three out of four evangelical Christians voted to return him to office.

## POLITICS & RELIGION IN CANADA

While it can be easy to see the mixing of religion and politics in the United States, not all of North America has the same religious focus. When it comes to religion and politics, the United States is in many ways unique among **Western** nations. Canada, by contrast, has less religious influence in its political realm.

## RELIGION & THE POLITICS OF WAR

Throughout history, religion has played a defining role in people's reasons for going to war and their attitudes toward violent conflict. For example, the Crusades of the eleventh through thirteenth centuries were military campaigns by Christian leaders and governments directed mostly against Muslims, but also against Jewish and other non-Christian populations. The Holocaust of the twentieth century primarily targeted the Jewish people of Western and Eastern Europe. The radical modern-day Jihad movement sees itself in a life-and-death struggle with the Western Christian world. Protestants and Catholics have fought for centuries in Northern Ireland.

The connection between religion and war, however, can be more complicated than one religious group fighting against another. For example, wars have been fought over the freedom to practice a certain religion—or people's religious beliefs may lead them to support wars that they believe are meant to liberate an oppressed group. In contrast, religions that advocate pacifism, such as the Quaker religion, teach that all war is unacceptable regardless of the reasons for which the war is fought.

*"Of all the tyrannies that affect mankind, tyranny in religion is the worst."*

—*Thomas Paine*

When it comes to the separation of church and state, these two North American nations appear quite similar. Sections 1 and 2 of the Canadian Charter of Rights and Freedoms state that certain freedoms are guaranteed and are subject "only to such reasonable limits prescribed by law as can be demonstrably justified in a free and democratic society." The charter lists freedom of religion among the guaranteed liberties, making this section of the charter similar to the First Amendment of the U.S. Constitution.

But while the two nations appear similar on paper, in practice there are definite differences. The United States is unusual as a technologically advanced yet religiously fervent nation, while Canada is more *secular*. Religioustolerance.org, a Web site operated by the Ontario (Canada) Consultants on Religious Tolerance, says, "perhaps there is no area of life in which differences are more noticeable [between the United States and Canada] than in the fields of religion and spirituality."

For one, Canada has very different religious *demographics* than the United States. In the United States, Protestants outnumber Catholics three to one. In Canada, however, Catholics outnumber Protestants by about 25 percent. There are also differences between Canadian and U.S. Protestantism. The largest Protestant group in the United States is the very *conservative* Southern Baptist Convention, while in Canada, the two largest Protestant church groups are the United Church of Canada and the Anglican Church of Canada, both noted for *liberal* beliefs.

According to religioustolerance.org, statistics on other religious affiliations show a similarity between the neighbors. Approximately 1.7 percent of Americans and 1.1 percent of Canadians declare Judaism as their religion. Islam is the religion of approximately 1.2 percent of U.S. residents and 2.0 percent of those living in Canada.

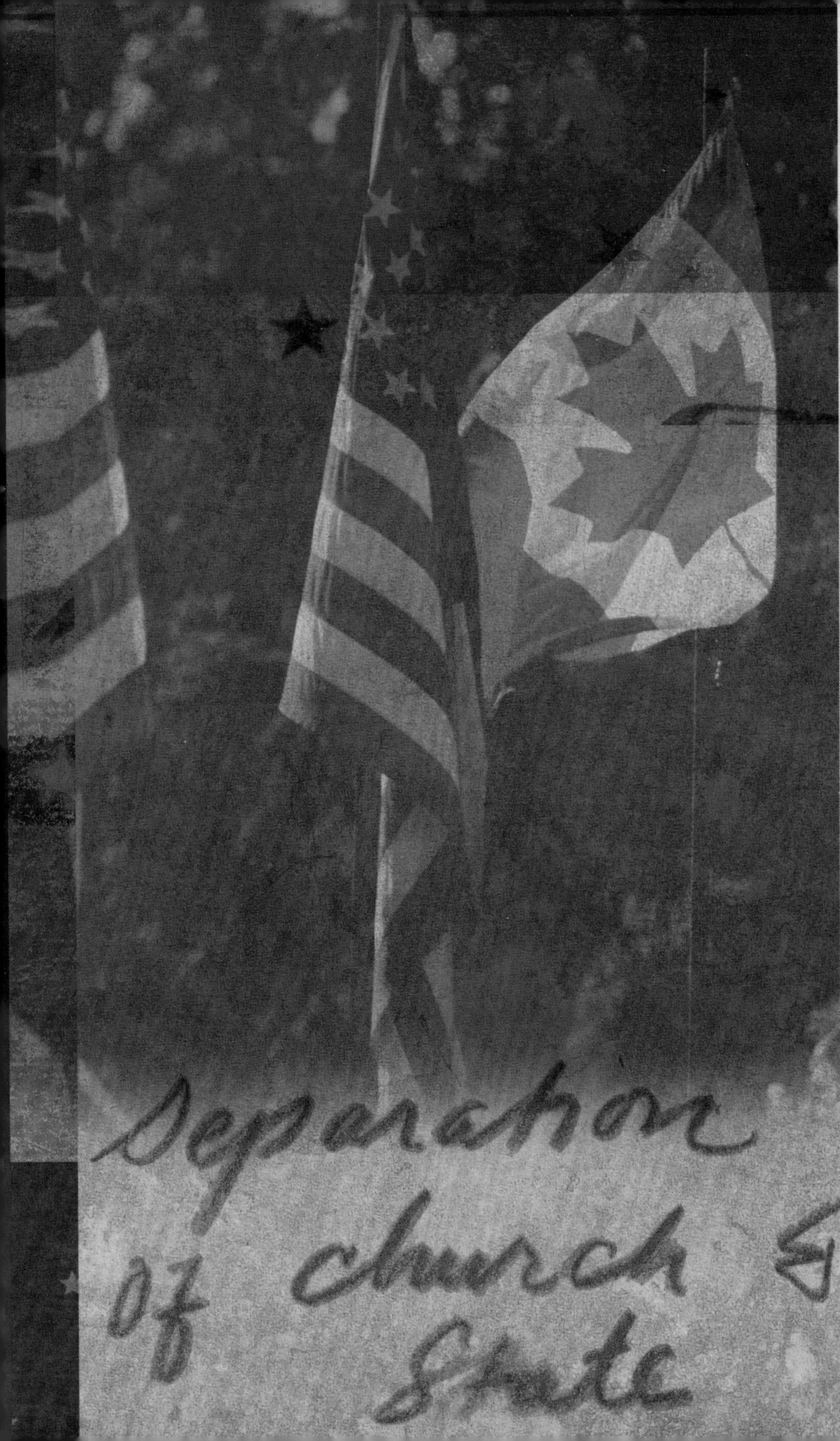
Separation
of church &
State

RELIGION & MODERN CULTURE

According to Statistics Canada's 2001 General Social Survey, religion plays an overall less prominent role in daily life in Canada than in the United States. Citizens in the United States are twice as likely to attend religious services regularly (43 percent in the United States as compared to 20 percent in Canada). Furthermore, the Taylor Nelson Sofres Intersearch (TNS) Millennium Study, conducted in 1999, found U.S. citizens are more likely to engage regularly in prayer or meditation (87 percent of all Americans compared to 68 percent of Canadians). Canadians, meanwhile, are twice as likely as U.S. citizens to consider themselves atheist or *agnostic*. However, many Canadians who are religious would be deeply offended by the idea that their religion is somehow less important or influential in their lives than it is for their U.S. counterparts. Religion may take a more public role in the United States than in Canada, but for many Canadian citizens, religion is still an immensely important part of their private lives.

Although today the United States may appear unique among Western nations in the public influence religion has, religion's influence on the American public and political realm is by no means new. Throughout U.S. history, religion has played a central role in shaping the nation both socially and politically. Events of the 1950s and 1960s may be some of the best examples of how religiously influenced social movements ultimately affected official government policy and changed the face of North America.

*Chapter 2*

RELIGION & MODERN CULTURE

# THE MARCH TO FREEDOM

It was the summer of 1964. Lyndon Johnson was the Democratic Party's nominee for the presidency. He wanted nothing to ruin his celebration. However, there was trouble brewing.

Fannie Lou Hamer, the founder of the Mississippi Freedom Democratic Party (MFDP), was rocking the boat. Mrs. Hamer, along with many other blacks in the country, was upset that all the Democratic delegates were white. She wanted blacks to have a say in the nomination. President Johnson sent Senator Hubert Humphrey, his future vice president, to talk to Mrs. Hamer to ask her what she wanted. She replied, "The beginning of a New Kingdom right here on earth."

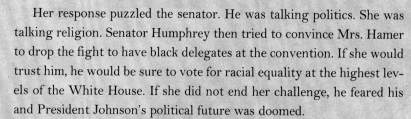

Her response puzzled the senator. He was talking politics. She was talking religion. Senator Humphrey then tried to convince Mrs. Hamer to drop the fight to have black delegates at the convention. If she would trust him, he would be sure to vote for racial equality at the highest levels of the White House. If she did not end her challenge, he feared his and President Johnson's political future was doomed.

In the book *God's Name in Vain*, Stephen L. Carter quotes Mrs. Hamer:

"Senator Humphrey, I know lots of people in Mississippi who have lost their jobs for trying to register to vote. I had to leave the plantation where I worked in Sunflower County. Now if you lose this job of vice president because you do what is right, because you help MFDP, everything will be all right. God will take care of you. But if you take [the vice presidential nomination] this way, why, you will never be able to do any good for civil rights, for poor people, for peace or any of those things you talk about. Senator Humphrey, I'm gonna pray to Jesus for you."

Senator Humphrey was looking to win an election. Mrs. Hamer was looking for justice, and her faith gave her a picture of what that justice should be. She and many other blacks in the United States were tired of **segregation**, of having to sit in the back of the bus, of being excluded from most restaurants, of having inferior schools, and of being denied the right to vote. The 1950s and 1960s brought a social movement more openly religious than any other: the civil rights movement. It was a movement fueled by a religious sense of vision. The theme of the movement was to follow the Bible's command to "love your neighbor." Preaching this theme, some of the greatest leaders America would know rose and changed the nation forever.

# GLOSSARY

**disillusioned**: Disappointed by or lost trust in a previously held belief.

**evangelist**: A person who preaches a religious message with the goal of converting others to his way of thinking.

**Hinduism**: The main religion of India. Hinduism is characterized by an ancient system of social divisions called the caste system and by belief in reincarnation.

**Koran**: The Islamic holy book, believed by Muslims to contain the revelations of Allah (the Muslim name for God) to Muhammad.

**militant**: Aggressive in the defense or support of a cause, often in a manner others find unacceptable.

**pilgrimage**: A religious journey to a holy place.

**provincial**: Having to do with the Canadian provinces, the administrative divisions of Canada that correspond to American states.

**secularization**: The process of changing something from a religious orientation to one that is nonreligious.

**segregation**: Forced separation of racial, ethnic, or gender groups.

**supremacist**: Characterized by beliefs that a particular group is superior to others and is entitled to dominate them.

*"In this land, our churches have always been sturdy defenders of the Constitutional and God-given rights of each citizen. We are politically free people because each of us is free to express his individual faith."*

*—President Dwight D. Eisenhower*

## DR. MARTIN LUTHER KING JR.

Dr. Martin Luther King Jr. was perhaps the most famous leader of the civil rights movement. He was a preacher before he was a reformer, and he followed the teachings of both Jesus and Mahatma Mohandas Gandhi. Gandhi's thinking was shaped by **Hinduism** and by the teachings of Jesus, and he taught **militant** nonviolence. Gandhi brought important changes to his nation of India, and he expressed the hope that American blacks would deliver the same message of nonviolent revolution to the world.

Inspired by Gandhi, King went on to start a revolution based on love, hope, and nonviolence. The Sermon on the Mount, found in the book of Matthew in the New Testament of the Christian Bible, was central to Dr. King's teachings. Many of his sermons and speeches revolved around this passage of the Bible, in which Jesus taught, "Blessed are the peacemakers: for they shall be called the children of God," "Judge not, that ye be not judged," and many other lessons.

Dr. King organized the Southern Christian Leadership Conference (SCLC). During the Birmingham, Alabama, campaign for civil rights, the SCLC asked followers to keep a pledge that contained ten points. The first commitment was to "Meditate daily on the teachings and life of Jesus." The third was "Walk and talk in the manner of Love, for God is Love."

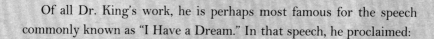

Of all Dr. King's work, he is perhaps most famous for the speech commonly known as "I Have a Dream." In that speech, he proclaimed:

I have a dream that one day this nation will rise up and live out the true meaning of its creed: "We hold these truths to be self-evident: that all men are created equal." I have a dream that one day on the red hills of Georgia the sons of former slaves and the sons of former slaveowners will be able to sit down together at a table of brotherhood. . . . I have a dream that my four children will one day live in a nation where they will not be judged by the color of their skin but by the content of their character. I have a dream today.

When we let freedom ring, when we let it ring from every village and every hamlet, from every state and every city, we will be able to speed up that day when all of God's children, black men and white men, Jews and Gentiles, Protestants and Catholics, will be able to join hands and sing in the words of the old Negro spiritual, "Free at last! free at last! thank God Almighty, we are free at last!" (Delivered August 28, 1963. Excerpt from *Martin Luther King Jr., The Peaceful Warrior.* New York: Pocket Books, 1968.)

Christian leaders weren't the only religious leaders involved in the civil rights movement. An important strength of the movement was that it relied on ideals that, though religiously or morally based, were not unique to one religion but rather shared by many religions. Many other religious leaders—from Jewish rabbis to Greek Orthodox priests—were involved in the movement.

But not all religious leaders approached the civil rights movement with the same commitment to nonviolence or goals of racial unity. For example, leaders of the Nation of Islam advocated a very different approach to achieving the rights that American blacks were being denied.

## SO IS IT MAHATMA OR MOHANDAS GANDHI?

The answer is—both. Mohandas Karamchand Gandhi is the great Indian leader's official name. Mahatma is a title of respect that he was given later in life. After graduating from law school, Gandhi took a position in South Africa. What started out as a one-year stay ended twenty years later. While in South Africa, Gandhi faced severe discrimination, as did many of the Indians living there in the late nineteenth and early twentieth centuries. Gandhi spent his years in South Africa working tirelessly to secure rights for the Indian population. His social action, based on the principles of courage, nonviolence, and truth (which he called *Satyagrha*), was in sharp contrast to the violence faced by the Indians living in a racially divided South Africa.

Gandhi's work in South Africa brought him worldwide attention. After Gandhi's return to his homeland, the people of India began referring to him as Mahatma, a term of great honor and respect. In India and Tibet, a mahatma is a title given to people who have uncommon knowledge of love and humanity. Gandhi's years of work in South Africa had shown his worthiness of the title. Soon he became Mahatma to the world.

*"Nonviolence is the greatest and most active force in the world."*

—*Mahatma Mohandas Gandhi*

## MALCOLM X

Like Martin Luther King Jr., Malcolm X's fight for equality was based on his faith. First, he rose as an important leader of the Nation of Islam. Later, his evolving religious beliefs would cause him to break from the Nation of Islam and ultimately lead to his murder.

The Nation of Islam had humble beginnings. In the summer of 1930, a light-skinned black man, Wallace D. Fard, began talking to blacks in a Detroit ghetto. He taught that the **Koran**, not the Bible, was the appropriate book for the black nation and argued that the white man had used Christianity to enslave black men.

Elijah Poole, who later became Elijah Muhammad, took over leadership of the movement after Fard disappeared. Muhammad declared himself "Prophet" and "Messenger of Allah." He taught that blacks must stop looking to whites for jobs and justice.

Meanwhile, Malcolm Little was serving a ten-year prison sentence for burglary. During his time at the Charlestown State Prison in Massachusetts, he first learned of the Nation of Islam, and it deeply affected his life. He spent his time in prison educating himself by reading and copying the entire dictionary. When he was released in 1952, he quickly became the Nation of Islam's top **evangelist**. This is when he took the name of Minister Malcolm X. Replacing one's family name with "X" was a common practice among members of the Nation of Islam. Many black Americans' family names have their origins in the names of white slaveholders—so for many in the Nation of Islam, the rejection of their family names showed a rejection of their slave past.

Malcolm X did not like the messages being spread by the black

## THE DEATH OF A DREAMER

At about 6:00 in the evening of April 4, 1968, in Memphis, Tennessee, Dr. Martin Luther King Jr., in the city for a rally to support striking sanitation workers, stepped onto the balcony of his second-story room at the Lorraine Motel. Dr. King and his friends stood chatting—until the night air was pierced by gunfire. In seconds, the man who preached nonviolence was dead, and Memphis and other parts of the United States erupted in rioting and looting.

James Earl Ray was arrested for the murder and confessed to the crime in court. Later he recanted his confession, saying that his fingerprints were on the gun because he had bought it for someone he knew only as "Raoul." Raoul was never identified or found, but Ray maintained his innocence until his death. Citing problems in the investigation, many people—including some members of Dr. King's family—no longer believe that James Earl Ray was the gunman.

Christian preachers of the time, which placed him against Dr. Martin Luther King Jr. He felt that the black preachers were in partnership with white men to keep blacks down. He believed that desegregation was one of their plans to harm blacks. Malcolm X believed that black

people must be united to end their oppression, and he felt that desegregation would only serve to further divide his people.

However, Malcolm X became ***disillusioned*** with the Nation of Islam, particularly with Elijah Muhammad, who was having extramarital affairs (which was strictly forbidden by the religion's teachings). In March 1964, Malcolm X left the Nation of Islam and took a ***pilgrimage*** to the Muslim holy city of Mecca. There he met representatives of mainstream Islam, and he was converted. He was especially impressed with their acceptance of all races. When he returned to the United States, he renounced the black ***supremacist*** teachings of the Nation of Islam, took El-Hajj Malik el-Shabazz as his new name, and began preaching principles of unity and freedom far more in line with other leaders of the civil rights movement.

Malcolm X had long been a controversial figure, considered dangerous by many white Americans. The Federal Bureau of Investigation (FBI) kept him under surveillance. However, his newly adopted beliefs put Malcolm X in even greater danger, for the Nation of Islam wanted him silenced. On February 2, 1965, three gunmen from the Nation of Islam shot and killed Malcolm X as he began a speech at the Audubon Ballroom in upper Manhattan.

## CÉSAR CHÁVEZ

Another champion for justice whose beliefs were guided by religious faith was César Estrada Chávez. Chávez is known for his work helping poor Latino migrant farmworkers. Born March 31, 1927, near Yuma, Arizona, to a family not rich by the world's standards, although he was rich in family love and connections. He learned compassion for others from seeing his family's generosity to those in need. His mother, Juana, made a policy of never turning away anyone in need of food.

In 1962, Chávez started the United Farm Workers (UFW). He made

## THE VIRGIN OF GUADALUPE

The Virgin of Guadalupe is an important figure for Catholic Latinos. According to tradition, she appeared in 1531 to an Aztec Indian named Juan Diego. The virgin had dark skin and spoke the Aztec language. Because she appeared to a simple peasant, not to the priests or the conquistadors, the Virgin of Guadalupe has been a unifying symbol for poor people struggling for their rights. In the 1960s, farmworkers protesting injustice used the Virgin of Guadalupe's image on their protest banners.

people aware of farmworkers' needs for better pay and safer working conditions. He used nonviolent tactics of boycotts, strikes, and pickets. Dignity was a key word for Chávez, and he wanted it for his people. He believed that through persistence, hard work, faith, and willingness to sacrifice, he and his followers could win justice. Several times he fasted for weeks to show his commitment to the cause.

Chávez depended on his faith, and he was influenced by the writings of Thomas Merton, a Catholic monk and pacifist. Many times, Chávez's companions wanted to turn to violence to achieve their demands, but he looked to Jesus's teachings and kept the cause on a nonviolent path.

In April 1993, César Chávez died in his sleep of natural causes at the age of sixty-six. At the time, he was defending his union in a court action, actively fighting for his people to the very end. More than 50,000

*Unlike most of the rest of Canada, Québec's population is mostly Roman Catholic.*

people came from across the United States to honor Chávez at his funeral. In 1994, President Bill Clinton awarded him the Presidential Medal of Freedom, the United States' highest honor for nonmilitary personnel. César's wife, Helen F. Chávez, accepted the award. César Chávez lives on in the hearts of many across America, and his influence continues.

## RELIGION & QUÉBEC'S QUIET REVOLUTION

During the 1960s, a social and political movement was also taking place in the Canadian province of Québec, a movement that would later be called the Quiet Revolution. In the United States, religious ideologies were fueling the civil rights movement, but during Québec's Quiet Revolution, a concerted effort was made to reduce religion's influence in politics.

Québec has a unique history in North America. During the colonial era, the French settled the area. Today, French is still the main language spoken in Québec, and some customs, traditions, and legal systems differ from those in the rest of Canada. Unlike most of the rest of Canada, Québec's population is mostly Roman Catholic.

Until the 1960s, the Catholic Church held more political power over Québec than has been typical of church–state relations in Canada and the United States. The politics, education, and economy of Québec were controlled by the very conservative Union Nationale party, which was strongly influenced by the Catholic Church. The Church controlled the province's educational system, and many felt that the Catholic Church

*faith*

and the Union Nationale were holding Québec back in its social, economic, and political development.

In the 1960 elections, the Liberal Party emerged as the majority in Québec. Under the Liberal Party's leadership, the province achieved the *secularization* of public education and widespread political and economic reforms. The Catholic Church, although still extremely important in private and public spheres in Québec, never regained the political influence it once held over the *provincial* government.

The separation of church and state is an important ideal in American and Canadian politics. At the same time, however, individuals like Fannie Lou Hamer, Dr. Martin Luther King Jr., Malcolm X, and César Chávez demonstrated that faith can be an important guiding principle for bringing about social and political change. In contrast, Québec's Quiet Revolution manifests some of the difficulties that can arise when a religion or religious body has a great deal of influence with the government.

Over the course of the twentieth century, similar conflicts and concerns regarding religion's influence on educational and political systems have arisen in the United States as well. Unlike Québec, where the Roman Catholic Church is the dominant religious force, in the United States, conservative Protestantism has had the most political influence, ultimately leading to the rise of what has been called Christian right-wing politics.

*Chapter 3*

RELIGION & MODERN CULTURE

# CHRISTIAN RIGHT-WING POLITICS

On a hot July day in 1925, reporters and curious onlookers crowded the courtroom in Dayton, Tennessee. For the first time in U.S. history, a trial was broadcast on radio live to the nation. The State of Tennessee was trying a high school biology teacher, John Thomas Scopes, for teaching evolution in a public school, an act that violated Tennessee law. One of the prosecuting attorneys was William Jennings Bryan. He wrote a popular weekly newspaper column on the Bible and was a leading figure in a religious movement called **fundamentalism**. One of the defense attorneys was Clarence Darrow. The public knew Darrow as a defender of "radicals" and as a well-known agnostic. Both men were nationally famous and bitter rivals. It would be hard to imagine a more sensational trial.

Darrow and the defense team's goal in the trial was not to have Scopes found innocent of teaching evolution: Scopes freely admitted doing such, and since teaching evolution was indeed illegal, he had clearly broken a law. For Darrow, Scopes, and the others involved, the antievolution law itself was on trial. They hoped the case would ultimately be brought before the U.S. Supreme Court and the antievolution law struck down as unconstitutional.

As the case progressed, it took on a carnival-like atmosphere, gathered huge crowds, and became a national media sensation. It was widely regarded as a battle between *modernists*, who believed that science and rationalism should govern intellectual inquiry, and fundamentalists, who believed not only that the Bible's teachings should be the authority on all matters but that everything in the Bible should be taken *literally*.

The most famous event of the trial occurred when, in a highly unusual move, prosecuting attorney William Jennings Bryan agreed to take the witness stand as a biblical expert. Darrow questioned Bryan on his literal interpretation of the Bible. Did he believe the sun actually stood still for Joshua? What would happen if the earth's rotation stopped suddenly? Bryan replied, "I don't think about things I don't think about." Darrow snapped back, "Do you think about things you do think about?" The crowd in the room chuckled.

Darrow moved on to question Bryan regarding the date of the earth's creation and the existence of a flood tradition in other ancient religions. Bryan stated he did not know about these things. Bryan complained, "The purpose [of this trial] is to cast ridicule on everyone who believes the Bible." Darrow argued, "We have the purpose of preventing bigots and ignoramuses from controlling the education of the United States."

Bryan won the case, and Scopes was fined $100.00. But Bryan's performance on the stand had been an embarrassment and made him appear less intelligent than his agnostic rival. Fundamentalism lost a considerable amount of credibility with the American public, and in the

# GLOSSARY

**activism**: Practice that includes getting involved, taking direct action to bring about a desired change in the surrounding world.

**counterculture**: A culture that has ideas and ways of behaving that are deliberately very different from the majority.

**fundamentalism**: A religious or political movement based on a literal and strict following of a doctrine.

**literally**: Based on the exact meaning of a word or text.

**modernists**: People who follow a tendency in theology to accommodate traditional religious teaching to contemporary thought and especially to devalue supernatural elements of religion.

**Right**: Political groups that support the established order and favor traditional attitudes and practices and conservative governmental policies (as opposed to the Left, which is liberal and progressive).

**socialists**: Believers in an economic and political system where the government owns much of the resources, so that wealth is distributed evenly among the entire population.

**subculture**: An identifiable social group within a larger culture.

44

H.I.V.

*"I think you do that [change society] by living out your faith with radical acts of compassion: by loving people who are H.I.V. [positive], by forming coalitions across ethnic and racial boundaries, by breaking down walls of racism, by extending love and compassion to the poor, by empowering people through opportunity. I know this all sounds like a social gospel, but to me it's the Gospel lived out in real life, and Jesus said, 'It's by your good works that they will glorify your Father Who is in Heaven.' I think we've forgotten that."*

—*Ed Dobson, former vice president of Moral Majority, Inc., sharing his more recent views of political involvement*

public's mind, there was now a great divide: the divide between science and conservative Christianity.

Following the Scopes trial of 1925, many American evangelicals separated themselves from the larger society. Karen Armstrong, a former nun and now a celebrated writer on religious topics, describes the trial's effects on conservative American Christianity:

Before the Scopes trial, fundamentalists had often been on the left of the political spectrum and had been willing to work alongside **socialists** and liberal Christians. . . . After the Scopes trial, they swung to the far right, where they remained. They felt humiliated by the media attack. It was very nasty. There was a sense of loss of prestige, and, above all, a sense of fear.

The stage was set at the presidential election of 1976 for change. The United States had just come through years of chaos. There had been the *counterculture* movement of the hippies, the war in Vietnam, the Watergate scandal, and the resignation of President Richard Nixon. Americans were ready for a candidate who was not a Washington insider.

At first, few people could believe it when a peanut farmer from Georgia declared his candidacy for the Democratic presidential nomination. He had been governor of Georgia for only one term, and not many outside of that state knew of him. What caught the eye of many churchgoing people was that he declared that he was a "born-again Christian." He even taught Sunday school at a Southern Baptist church in his hometown of Plains, Georgia. In Randall Balmer's book *Religion in Twentieth Century America*, he says the novelty of an evangelical Christian running for president entranced the media: "*Newsweek* magazine declared 1976 'the year of the Evangelical.'"

Once elected, President Carter enjoyed the support of politically conservative Christians for some time. However, a little-known incident turned away a large group of these supporters. Carter's justice department tried to enforce antidiscrimination laws at Bob Jones University, a fundamentalist college in Greenville, South Carolina. Based on their particular religious beliefs, Bob Jones University (BJU) prohibited interracial dating. The Internal Revenue Service (IRS) attempted to revoke the school's tax-exempt privilege, a privilege extended to religious institutions. The IRS said BJU must follow U.S. laws against discrimination in order to be tax exempt. The school fought the decision in the courts, but in 1983, the Supreme Court ruled against BJU.

By then, Ronald Reagan had become president. He defended the university, but the Court ruled that religious institutions had to follow the nation's laws against racial discrimination in order to enjoy benefits granted by the federal government. Fundamentalist Christians saw the federal

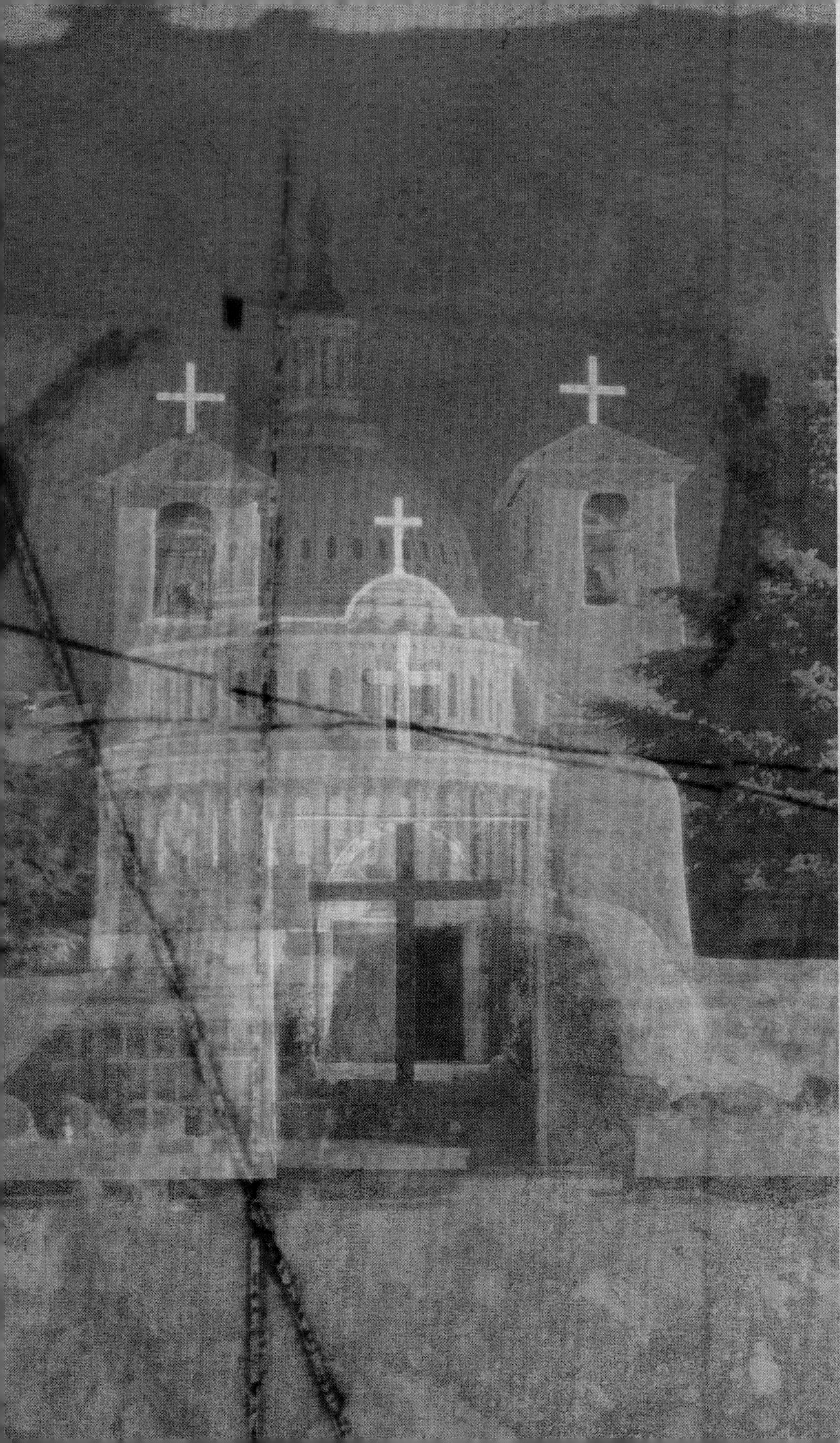

# CHRISTIAN RIGHT-WING POLITICS

moral majority

*"If warfare and violence become endemic in a society, religion gets sucked right into that. Religion comes from where our dreams come from, and if our dreams become disturbed, everything about us becomes disturbed in times of war and violence."*

—author Karen Armstrong, speaking about the Religious Right

government as intruding into their **subculture**. For many years, they had isolated themselves in their own institutions and taught what they wanted to teach. Now they felt the government was trying to tell them what they could and could not do.

## THE MORAL MAJORITY

The ruling in the BJU case motivated conservative Christians to become politically involved to keep the federal government from controlling what they saw as moral and religious issues. In 1979, Jerry Falwell, a conservative Baptist minister, formed a group called the Moral Majority. Other organizations with similar beliefs were Focus on the Family, the Religious Roundtable, Concerned Women for America, and Traditional Values Coalition. The Moral Majority and others on the religious **Right** believed the federal government, through the passage of laws such as those that allowed abortion, protected the rights of homosexuals, and other similar policies, was institutionalizing and promoting immorality. They believed Christians, for the good of the country and the souls of the nation, needed to "take back" the government and reinsert their moral and religious values into American public life and policy.

## PAT ROBERTSON

During the 1970s, several evangelical preachers gained publicity for their television broadcasts. One of these was Marion G. "Pat" Robertson. He bought a television station in 1961 and began broadcasting religious programs three hours a night. He called the station the Christian Broadcasting Network (CBN).

On September 17, 1986, Robertson announced his candidacy for the Republican presidential nomination. He stated that he wanted three million signatures showing support. He got them thanks to his CBN exposure. He then left CBN and resigned from his Southern Baptist ordination. Roberts tried to get away from his televangelist image but was not very successful. In the end, George H. W. Bush won the nomination. Although Robertson did not win, he helped to bring many other evangelicals into political activity.

One of these men was Ralph Reed. Robertson met him at the inauguration for George H. W. Bush. Reed helped Robertson transform the Christian followers he had assembled during his campaign into a political voting force for conservative evangelicals. Together they started the Christian Coalition. With more than a million followers, this group became a major force in American politics, especially within the Republican Party.

## THE LESSENING INFLUENCE
## OF THE RELIGIOUS RIGHT IN 2000

By the end of the twentieth century, the power of the Religious Right appeared to have declined. In the 2000 presidential election, six million conservative evangelical voters stayed home. Their failure to vote may

have prevented George W. Bush from winning the popular vote. What had gone wrong with the religious conservative movement?

Authors Cal Thomas and Ed Dobson explore this question in their book *Blinded by Might*. Both men worked for the Moral Majority, and their experiences in Christian political **activism** left them disillusioned. Thomas and Dobson believe their experiment of transforming America through the Moral Majority failed.

Dobson and Thomas suggest that when preachers become political, "they are often seduced by the siren song of temporal political power." The world of politics, they say, is often corrupt. When religious leaders set their sights on power, they too often lower their standards for personal behavior. Rather than focus on political power, Dobson and Thomas say that conservative Christians should continue to put their trust in the power of faith. Dobson says, "I now believe that the way to transform our nation has little to do with politics and everything to do with offering people the gospel."

# THE RELIGIOUS RIGHT IS STILL INFLUENTIAL IN 2004

The 2004 election suggests conservative Christians still hold substantial political power in the United States, however. Dr. James Dobson (not to be confused with Ed Dobson), the host of the conservative Christian radio talk show *Focus on the Family*, urged conservative Christians to vote and oppose gay marriage. They did so, banning the practice in the eleven states that brought the issue to the ballot. Just before the November 2 election, surveys showed Senator John Kerry and President George W. Bush in a tie for the presidency. On Election Day, however, President Bush won a second term.

In the days following the election, several political analysts pointed to one difference between the candidates: religious faith. Kerry spoke of his Catholic beliefs as important to him, but he did not use the sort of direct religious language in which the president spoke. Voters said the most important factor for them on Election Day was "moral values," which includes religious values. A majority of voters who identified themselves as evangelical voted for Bush. All this suggests that the Religious Right continues to play a strong role in American politics.

The 2004 election, however, did not only show that morality and religion in general were important to voters. It also showed that certain specific "moral" issues were more important than others. Throughout the campaign, debates were raised about a number of issues that are heavily influenced by individuals' moral and religious beliefs, among them abortion, stem-cell research, and same-sex marriage. Despite the fact that the U.S. Supreme Court ruled on the issue decades ago, abortion continues to be one of the most politically influential moral issues in America. In recent years, stem-cell research has joined abortion in a political fray where religiously influenced beliefs regarding life and its legal protection are hotly debated.

## CHRISTIAN ALTERNATIVES
## TO THE POLITICAL RIGHT

During the 1980s, some Christians disagreed with the Moral Majority and other Christian right-wing political groups. For example, unlike the conservatives, these Christians opposed the increasing U.S. arsenal of nuclear weapons. They were also deeply concerned with conservative approaches to dealing with poverty. Ronald Reagan and Christian Republican supporters pushed for what they called "trickle-down" economics. They believed that by reducing welfare benefits and aiding big businesses, the economy would become stronger and the newly created wealth would work its way down the social ladder, eventually allowing poor people to lift themselves above poverty. Some Christians, however, believed these policies neglected and harmed the poor. Evangelical and Catholic activists who thought of themselves as "progressive" Christians recalled how Christians in the 1800s had freed slaves, established hospitals, and cared for the poor. Jim Wallace started a Christian community in inner-city Washington, D.C., named Sojourners. Ronald Sider established Evangelicals for Social Action. These and other groups turned church basements into homeless shelters, protested nuclear weapons, and pressured politicians to seek justice for the poor.

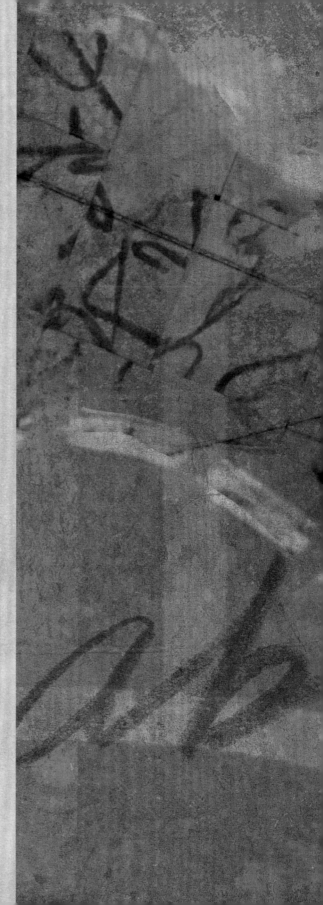

# Chapter 4

# ABORTION

It was August of 1969, and Norma McCorvey loved her new job selling tickets to a carnival sideshow. Her new friends made her feel like part of a family. She had no idea that her life would soon change forever. She was about to be thrown into the middle of one of America's greatest controversies.

After a long night's work, McCorvey and two friends were walking back to their motel when they were attacked. The attackers raped McCorvey. She woke up alone on the street and stumbled back to her motel room. The next morning, her roommates were gone, and so was the carnival. Penniless, she returned to Dallas, where her family and some friends lived. As the weeks passed, McCorvey realized she was pregnant. She was too poor to raise a baby on her own. Her parents had divorced and were not supportive, and she did not even know who the father was.

This is the story Norma McCorvey told in 1969. She was pregnant after having consensual sex with her boyfriend. This lie would only be corrected decades later.

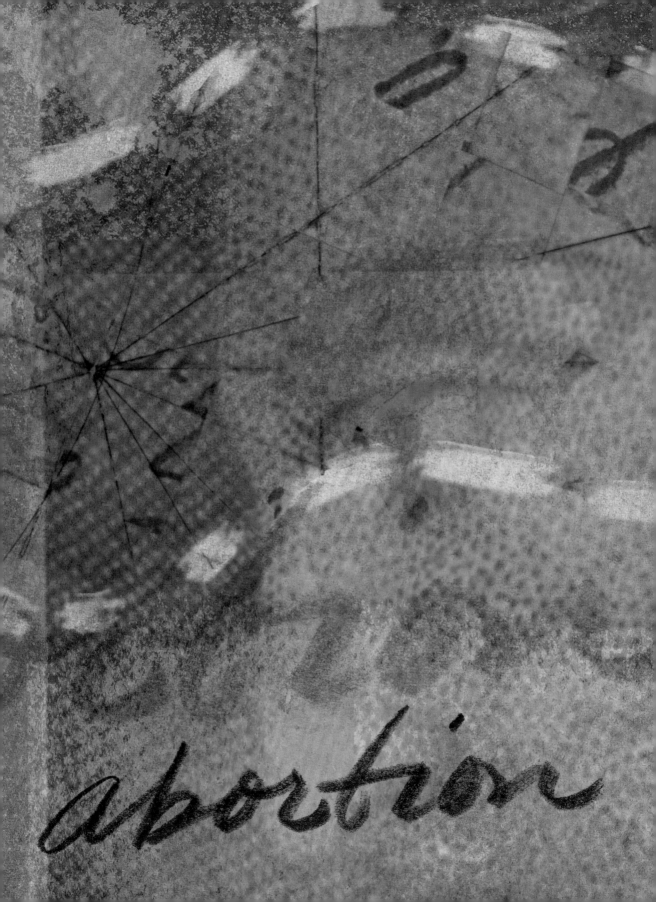

McCorvey thought about having an abortion, but they were illegal in Texas. She went to her physician and explained her circumstances, but her doctor refused to help. McCorvey thought of having an illegal abortion, but the stories of unsafe and disastrous operations were too frightening.

Norma McCorvey then got in touch with Linda Coffee and Sarah Weddington, two lawyers who were looking for a person who would bring an abortion lawsuit against the State of Texas to change its laws. McCorvey was willing to make such a case. However, she was afraid of her family knowing of her decision to have an abortion. Weddington and Coffee had the idea of creating a false name to protect McCorvey. They called her Jane Roe.

On June 17, 1970, the Fifth Circuit Court in New Orleans, Louisiana, ruled that the Texas abortion law was unconstitutional. The court stated that the privacy of a woman should be protected; she should be able to decide what to do with her body. But there was a loophole in the court's ruling. They did not issue an *injunction* against the state, so Texas could still enforce their antiabortion law. McCorvey would still be unable to get an abortion. Coffee and Weddington made an appeal to the U.S. Supreme Court.

The Supreme Court struggled with the decision for several years. During this time, Norma McCorvey carried her baby to term and put the child up for adoption. Though the ruling would be too late for her, she was intent on fighting for the cause of abortion. Finally, on January 22, 1973, the Court delivered their opinion. Judge Harry A. Blackmun addressed the courtroom. He expressed the Court's "awareness of the sensitive and emotional nature of the abortion controversy. . . . One's philosophy, one's experiences, . . . one's religious training, one's attitudes toward life . . . are all likely to influence and to color one's thinking and conclusions about abortion." The Court went on to state that a woman had a right to an abortion.

On the day the Supreme Court gave its ruling, former president Lyndon Johnson died. This pushed the news of *Roe v. Wade* from the

# GLOSSARY

**ambivalent**: Having mixed, uncertain, or conflicting feelings about something.

**fetus**: A developing or unborn human during the period between eight weeks after conception and birth. Many who are pro-choice prefer this term as being less emotionally charged, while many who are pro-life use "baby" to affirm their beliefs in the humanity of the unborn.

**incest**: Sexual relations between people who are related.

**injunction**: A court order requiring someone involved in a legal action to do something or refrain from doing something.

**Pentecostal**: Relating to Protestant churches that emphasize the individual experience of God's grace demonstrated through such spiritual gifts as speaking in tongues, faith healing, and other miracles, as well as with emotional and expressive worship service.

**sanctity**: The quality of being holy, sacred.

Roe v. Wade

*"I am dedicated to spending the rest of my life un-
doing the law that bears my name. I would like
nothing more than to have this law overturned."*

—*Norma L. McCorvey ("Jane Roe" of* Roe v. Wade*)*

headlines of the newspapers. At home in Texas, Norma McCorvey read
about the victory in her local newspaper and burst into tears. A friend
staying with her, seeing the headlines about Johnson, asked if Norma
had known the president. "No," she explained, "I'm Jane Roe."

In 1987, Norma McCorvey confessed to *Washington Times* writer
Carl Rowan that her account of the 1969 rape was a lie. She told her
false story in hope of invalidating the law against abortion. The *Roe* decision was based on a lie. Sarah Weddington, her lawyer, claims the
issue of rape was not brought up in the case. The deciding factor in *Roe
v. Wade* was whether the U.S. Consitution gives the state the right to
decide what a woman can do with her body.

Religious leaders had mixed reactions to the *Roe v. Wade* decision.
The president of the National Catholic Conference, John Cardinal Krol,
declared that the Court had now opened the doors to the "greatest
slaughter of innocent life in the history of mankind." Other religious
groups were **ambivalent**—and in some cases welcoming—of the *Roe v.
Wade* decision.

## PUBLIC BELIEFS REGARDING ABORTION

Perhaps no issue is as controversial and divisive in American politics
and society as that of abortion. For some people, the abortion issue is
quite simple: a *fetus* cannot live outside a woman's body and consequently must be considered part of her body: people have the right to
make their own decisions about their bodies, so women have the right
to decide whether or not to have an abortion. Other people see the issue

as equally black and white from the opposite viewpoint: a fetus is a human being, and it is morally wrong to take human life; the unborn child's life must consequently be legally protected. Still others see the issue as far more complicated. Often religious beliefs influence various and conflicting perspectives.

Arguments for and against abortion involve complex questions. When does human life begin? Does life begin at conception, at a later stage of fetal development, or at birth? Does a fetus have a right to life? How does one weigh the needs of the fetus with the needs of the pregnant woman? Are there cases where abortions are a necessary option—such as pregnancy from rape or incest, severe deformity in the fetus, or medical risk to the mother? Who should have the right to make a choice for or against abortion—the state or the pregnant woman?

U.S. citizens hold a variety of beliefs regarding abortion. A Gallup poll in 2000 found Americans evenly divided when asked if they were "pro-life" or "pro-choice." Forty-six percent said they were pro-life, and exactly the same number said they supported women's right to choose.

However, more detailed questions show that only a minority of U.S. citizens have hard-line positions on either side of the abortion debate. Only one in four U.S. citizens says abortion should be legal in all cases, while only 15 percent of Americans say abortion should be illegal in all cases. The majority holds "in-between" views. Slightly more than 40 percent say abortion should be legal only in certain cases, and the remaining 14 percent say it should be legal in most cases.

Canadian citizens also hold a complex set of views on the issue. A 2002 Leger Marketing survey asked Canadians, "At what point during human development should the law protect human life?" The results showed that 37 percent favored protection from conception on. Thirteen percent believe protection should begin after three months gestation. Six percent believed protection should begin after six months. Thirty percent said there should be no legal protection until after birth.

Unlike the United States, Canada has no laws limiting abortions. Provincial medical associations do, however, have regulations that restrict late-term abortions. Although more than 40 percent of Canadians are members of the Roman Catholic Church, which officially opposes legalized abortion, Canada has not seen large-scale religious protests like those organized by Operation Rescue and the Moral Majority in the United States.

## A DOCTOR'S CHOICE

Curtis Boyd preached in his Baptist church as a youth. He became a medical doctor in the early 1960s, and members of a national organization called Clergy Consultation on Problem Pregnancy approached Dr. Boyd in 1965. The Clergy Consultation was a group of religious leaders from many backgrounds whose religious beliefs led them to support access to abortions. They were concerned about the growing number of women who were too poor to obtain safe abortions and who were injured or even killed from unsafe, illegal procedures. For these religious leaders, denying women access to abortion seemed morally reprehensible.

The group provided women with referrals to doctors who were willing to provide abortion services. Dr. Boyd was hesitant to do illegal surgery, yet he felt it was important to provide a safe alternative to dangerous, back-alley abortions. Because of his moral and religious beliefs on the issue, Boyd risked imprisonment and loss of his medical license to provide abortions.

*"Keep your rosaries off my ovaries"*
—*from a sign at a pro-choice rally*

## RELIGIOUS BELIEFS REGARDING ABORTION

Religious groups in North America hold a variety of views regarding legalized abortion. Some opposing groups are Roman Catholics, the
Southern Baptist Convention, and the Assemblies of God. They believe
that a fetus is a human being from the moment of conception and that
ending a human life is always wrong no matter what the circumstances.
Other large denominations, such as the United Methodists,
Presbyterians, Lutherans, and American Baptists believe abortion may be
morally justified in certain cases. They believe the scriptures require that
the needs of the pregnant woman as well as the fetus be considered.

Most Christian denominations oppose "abortion for convenience,"
such as having an abortion because of an accidental, undesired, pregnancy. They teach that abortion should be considered only when other
issues, such as the physical or mental health of the mother, make such a
choice necessary. At the same time, the majority of Christian churches
hold that issues of justice and health for the mother, or quality of life for
the child, may make abortion an unfortunate yet morally defendable
choice. They would say that abortion is never a "good" action, but sometimes it is the best one of two unattractive alternatives.

Christian leaders also hold a variety of views regarding the legality
of abortion. Some who oppose abortion in most cases nevertheless defend the right of women to make that choice themselves, rather than
have that choice defined by the state. Thus, they support *Roe v. Wade*
while regretting that some women choose abortions lightly or unwisely.

Roman Catholic leaders are categorically opposed to abortion.
Catholics believe a fetus is a human being from the moment of conception, and the Roman Catholic Church teaches that all abortions are a
form of murder, no matter what the situation or conditions leading to

the pregnancy. The Church also believes that governments must give fetuses the same legal protections they give all human beings. They base this understanding on their interpretation of scripture and on their interpretation of early Christian beliefs.

However, the leaders of the Catholic Church do not represent the views of average Catholic believers in the United States. In 1992, the Gallup organization surveyed Catholic citizens regarding abortion. The survey concluded that even among U.S. Catholics who attend church each week, most reject the Church's position that abortion should be illegal in all circumstances. Thirty-one percent said it should be legal either in "many" or in "all" cases, and 45 percent said it should be legal in rare circumstances. Only 22 percent of American Catholics surveyed agreed with the official Church position that abortion should be illegal in all circumstances.

The Southern Baptist Convention also teaches that human life begins at conception. In the past, it taught that abortion would be a legitimate moral choice under difficult circumstances. In June of 1971, before

## ONE CHRISTIAN'S VIEW

Tony Campolo is an American Baptist professor of sociology at Eastern College and an evangelist who is especially popular with youth. Campolo says he regrets that some politically conservative Christians have made opposition to abortion a test of genuine faith. Campolo personally stands "against abortion, especially in terms of late-term abortions, but I am not willing to say those who differ with me are not Christians." He hopes that "the discussion between pro-life and pro-choice Christians can continue with civility rather than with the name-calling that I too often hear from both sides on this hot and extremely important issue."

the *Roe v. Wade* decision, the Southern Baptist Convention passed a resolution urging the state to legalize abortion "under such conditions as rape, **incest**, clear evidence of severe fetal deformity, and . . . likelihood of damage to the emotional, mental, and physical health of the mother." More recently, however, it has changed its views. A June 1991 resolution urged repeal of *Roe v. Wade* and stated, "We affirm the biblical prohibition against the taking of unborn human life except to save the life of the mother."

The Assembly of God, the largest **Pentecostal** Christian group in North America, states,

The Assembly of God is unashamedly pro-life. Even though a United States Supreme Court decision legalized abortion in 1973, abortion is still immoral and sinful. This stand is founded on the biblical truth that all human life is created in the image of God (Genesis 1:27). From that truth issues the long-standing Christian view that aborting the life of a developing child is evil.

Mainstream churches—large, well-established denominations with a long history in America—teach that abortion is sometimes necessary but generally an undesirable moral choice. The American Baptists hold this view:

> we oppose abortion, as a means of avoiding responsibility for conception, as a primary means of birth control, and without regard for the far-reaching consequences of the act. . . . We grieve with all who struggle with the difficult circumstances that lead them to consider abortion. Recognizing that each person is ultimately responsible to God, we encourage men and women in these circumstances to seek spiritual counsel as they prayerfully and conscientiously consider their decision.

In 1991, the Evangelical Lutheran Church in America (ELCA) issued a statement reading,

> A developing life in the womb does not have an absolute right to be born, nor does a pregnant woman have an absolute right to terminate a pregnancy. The concern for both the life of the woman and the developing life in her womb expresses a common commitment to life.

They believe "Abortion ought to be an option only of last resort." At the same time, the ELCA teaches, "This church recognizes that there can be sound reasons for ending a pregnancy through induced abortion." The Presbyterian Church (USA) likewise says, "Abortion should be the choice of last resort in cases of problem pregnancy."

The United Methodist Church teaches,

> Our belief in the *sanctity* of unborn human life makes us reluctant to approve abortion. But we are equally bound to respect the sacredness of the life and well-being of the mother, for whom devastating damage may result from an unacceptable pregnancy. In continuity with past Christian teaching, we recognize tragic conflicts of life with life that may justify abortion, and in such cases we support the legal option of abortion under proper medical procedures.

Judaism does not regard a fetus as "a full human being," yet still urges women to avoid abortion unless there are harmful circumstances to the pregnancy. Rabbi Raymond A. Zwerin and Rabbi Richard J. Shapiro, writing for the Religious Coalition for Reproductive Choice, say,

> just as any person may not voluntarily do harm to his or her body, a woman may not voluntarily abort a fetus. However, just as a portion of the body may be sacrificed to save a person's life, an abortion may be performed for the woman's overall well-being, and an existing life takes precedence over a potential life, if there must be a choice between them.

## NORMA McCORVEY: THE SECOND HALF OF A COMPLICATED STORY

On March 31, 1995, a group called Operation Rescue rented an office in north Dallas, Texas, next to A Choice for Women, an abortion clinic. There were many conflicts between Operation Rescue staff and clinic

## PRO-LIFE: A LARGER ISSUE?

Many religious leaders believe being pro-life goes beyond opposing abortion. They regard the rights and health of all persons—not just the unborn—as important. Glen Stassen is professor of Christian Ethics at Fuller Theological Seminary in Pasadena, California. Stassen considers himself pro-life, but the policies of the Bush administration trouble the professor. While President Bush is a strong opponent of abortion, Stassen believes the president's policies in other areas undercut his concern for life. He says that increased poverty, along with cuts in medical care and education, have caused more women in the United States to seek abortions. Stassen teaches,

> Economic policy and abortion are not separate issues; they form one moral imperative. Rhetoric is hollow, mere tinkling brass, without health care, health insurance, jobs, childcare, and a living wage. Pro-life in deed, not merely in word, means we need a president who will do something about jobs and insurance and support for prospective mothers.

# THE EXTREMES OF
# THE ANTIABORTION MOVEMENT

In 1986, Randall Terry of Binghamton, New York, began Operation Rescue, and it has been one of the most publicized antiabortion Christian groups. Operation Rescue believes that aggressive but nonviolent protests are necessary in order to save unborn lives. They blockade abortion clinics, parking their cars around the clinic and preventing women from entering. Sometimes they sit or lie down in front of the clinic, achieving the same effect. The government has ruled it is illegal to blockade clinics and has arrested many "rescuers" on charges of criminal trespass. A number have spent time in jail for opposing abortion.

Operation Rescue, however, is by no means the most extreme in the antiabortion movement. Others have resorted to violence, participating in arson and bombings of clinics, causing millions of dollars worth of damage, threatening doctors who perform abortions, and even murdering some doctors and health-care professionals. Most antiabortionists oppose such actions.

*Many religious leaders believe being pro-life goes beyond opposing abortion. They regard the rights and health of all persons—not just the unborn—as important.*

workers. One of the workers was especially aggressive toward the antiabortionists. She was Norma McCorvey, Jane Roe.

Over the months that Operation Rescue worked beside the clinic, occasional conversations took place between the two sides. McCorvey began speaking more calmly with the Operation Rescue staff, and some unlikely friendships began. She became friends with seven-year-old Emily, the daughter of Ronda Mackey, one of the volunteers. On her Roe no More Ministry Web site, McCorvey tells what happened during the following months.

Emily began to personify the issue of abortion for McCorvey, especially when Ronda Mackey told her that she had almost aborted Emily. McCorvey says, "Abortion was no longer an abstract right. It had a face now, in a little girl named Emily." McCorvey attended church one day with the Mackeys because Emily begged her to come. She says she turned her life over to God at that church. Her new beliefs caused her to change her view on abortion. She now declares herself pro-life. Norma McCorvey has been the test case for legalizing abortion, an avid abortion proponent, and now she is an opponent of abortion because of her Christian beliefs. Her life illustrates the wide variety of emotional and spiritual factors surrounding this complicated issue.

As Norma McCorvey's story also illustrates, the issues surrounding abortion have no easy answers. No one expects the public and private debates to end any time soon. And recent advances in the medical field have pushed debates concerning fetal life further into the public realm. Like abortion, stem-cell research has become a controversial topic strongly influenced by issues of morality and religion.

# Chapter 5

## STEM-CELL RESEARCH

RELIGION & MODERN CULTURE

Christopher Reeve was the star of the *Superman* movies, but for many Americans, he also became a real-life hero. In 1995, a horseback-riding accident left Reeve paralyzed from the neck down. His old friend Senator John Kerry mentioned Reeve's name in the second presidential debate with President Bush in October of 2004. The issue on the table was stem-cell research. Reeve, Kerry, and a multitude of others had spent years fighting a battle over this heated topic.

Stem-cell research

Stem-cell research is a field of medicine that may prove helpful for treating conditions in which body cells have died, become diseased, or malfunctioned. When the body is functioning normally, old or unhealthy cells are replaced through cell division; for example, one skin cell multiplies and divides into two new skin cells. Normally, cells can only come from like cells: a skin cell can only come from a skin cell, a lung cell can only come from a lung cell, a brain cell can only come from a brain cell, and so on. So what happens if all of one type of cell in the body becomes sick or dies? Where will the new, healthy cells come from? Stem cells have great potential for *therapeutic* treatments because they are undifferentiated, meaning they are not yet a specific type of body cell; they can be triggered to develop into different types of cells. For example, an embryonic stem cell (a stem cell that comes from an *embryo*) could become a brain, pancreatic, liver, lung, or heart cell. Some of the diseases and conditions that stem cells might be able to treat or cure are diabetes, *Alzheimer's disease, Parkinson's disease,* and spinal cord injuries.

Stem cells have a number of sources. Adult stem cells exist in bone marrow. When a baby is born, stem cells exist in the *umbilical cord* and *placenta*. Both adult stem cells and stem cells from umbilical cords and placentas have potential for medical treatments. However, many scientists believe that embryonic stem cells have the most potential for therapeutic treatments because they can become almost any body tissue. Adult stem cells may only be able to become cells of the type of tissue from which they originate.

The stem cells used in embryonic stem-cell research (ESCR) come from embryos left over after a process called in vitro fertilization. In vitro fertilization is a fertility treatment that helps many people who have difficulty conceiving children. Eggs are taken from the woman, and sperm is taken from the man. The eggs are fertilized outside the woman's body, and the resulting embryos are implanted directly into her uterus. In vitro fertilization has a high failure rate, so many couples must undergo the treatment more than once before a successful preg-

# GLOSSARY

**Alzheimer's disease**: A degenerative disorder of later life that affects the brain and causes dementia.

**embryo**: The developing offspring between conception and the end of the eighth week.

**Parkinson's disease**: A nervous disorder characterized by trembling hands, lifeless face, monotone voice, and a shuffling walk.

**placenta**: An organ inside the uterus that develops during pregnancy and supplies food and oxygen to the fetus via the umbilical cord.

**therapeutic**: Used in the treatment of disease or disorders.

**umbilical cord**: The tube connecting the fetus to the placenta through which nutrients are delivered and waste is expelled.

**viable**: Able to live, function, or develop.

nancy occurs. Because of this, more embryos are created than will be implanted into the woman. The extras are frozen to be used later if the first implantation is not successful. In most cases, the extras are frozen indefinitely, and many are eventually thrown out. Many couples have decided to donate their extra embryos to ESCR rather than have them thrown out. Researchers remove the stem cells from the inner cell mass, harvesting the stem cells but destroying the rest of the embryo. Under proper conditions, these stem cells can be multiplied and grown into a stem-cell line.

## RELIGIOUS BELIEFS & STEM-CELL RESEARCH

Americans support stem-cell research by a two-to-one margin and in general support federal funding for such research. An ABC News poll taken in June of 2004 found that among white evangelical Christians in the United States, 50 percent support ESCR, while 40 percent oppose it. Even among those evangelicals who said they were opponents of legal abortion, opposition to stem-cell research fell to just short of a majority.

Some of the same religious groups that have opposed legalized abortion oppose ESCR for similar reasons. James Dobson of Focus on the Family writes, "In order for scientists to isolate and culture embryonic stem cells, a living, human embryo must be killed. . . . By requiring the destruction of embryos, the tiniest human beings, embryonic stem cell research violates the medical ethic of 'Do No Harm.'" Surveys indicate that statements by Dobson and some other politically conservative leaders have not convinced the majority of evangelicals to oppose ESCR.

The Catholic Church also opposes ESCR. In *Newsweek*'s issue of October 25, 2004, Richard Doerflinger of the U.S. Conference of Catholic Bishops says, "There are elements to this agenda that make it even more serious than abortion. You have the prospect of creating lives

> *"You really don't have an ethical problem [with stem-cell research] because you're actually saving lives by using cells that are going into the garbage. I just don't see how that's immoral or unethical. I really don't."*
>
> —Christopher Reeve

just to destroy them." However, opposition to ESCR by Church leaders has not convinced the majority of American Catholics. The June 2004 ABC poll also found that 54 percent of Catholics support ESCR, while 35 percent are opposed; 60 percent support its federal funding, while just 32 percent oppose such funding.

In 2004, Lisa and Jack Reed Jr. of the First United Methodist Church in Tupelo, Mississippi, presented a petition titled "People of Faith for Stem Cell Research" to President Bush. The Reed's son, Jack Reed III, has juvenile diabetes. In 2001, they joined 104 other families from Mississippi and Alabama in writing a letter from "people of faith," asking that President Bush expand the current federal policy on embryonic stem-cell research. By summer of 2004, more than nine thousand people of faith had signed the petition, including prominent pastors, priests, rabbis, and theologians.

The petition affirms,

> Many of our faith traditions teach an obligation to pursue research that promotes healing and diminishes suffering. In keeping with these traditions, we believe that embryonic stem cell research is a legitimate domain of inquiry and is consistent with the principle of full respect for human life.

This petition echoes the beliefs of many religious people that the commandment "Thou shall not kill" does not just prohibit violence. They

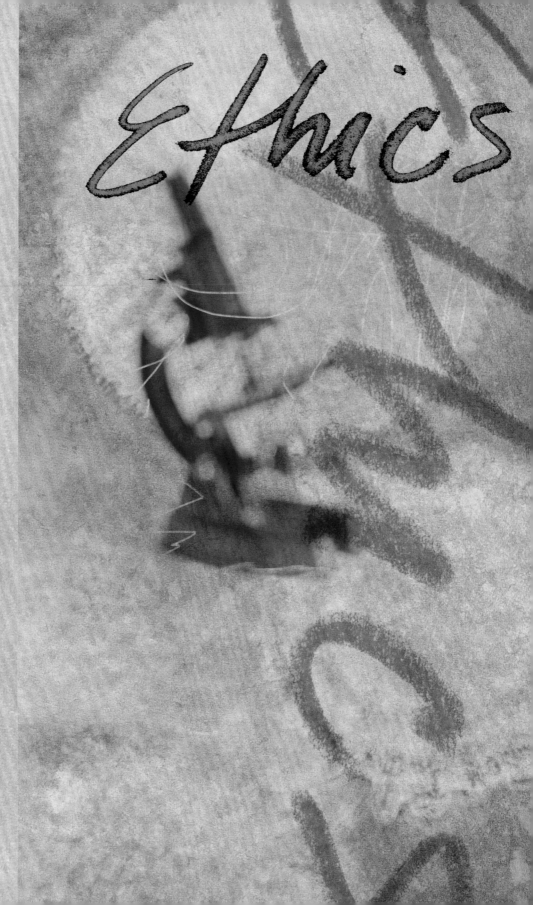

Ethics

RELIGION & MODERN CULTURE

*"The issue is debated within the church, with people of different faiths, even many of the same faith coming to different conclusions. Many people are finding that the more they know about stem cell research, the less certain they are about the right ethical and moral conclusions."*

—*President George W. Bush, August 9, 2001*

believe the commandment also requires that people take positive action to nurture health and strengthen life.

In August 2001, President Bush signed an order to restrict ESCR. The restriction allows research to continue on the stem-cell lines currently in existence (there are estimated to be more than sixty stem-cell lines currently in existence), but bans the creation of any new stem-cell lines derived from embryos. Scientists who want to study embryonic stem cells can pay about $5,000 and have a cluster of frozen cells sent to them from one of the existing lines. Unfortunately, there are many problems with the existing lines, and only a small number of them are *viable* for research purposes.

Many scientists, celebrities, religious leaders, and the Coalition for the Advancement of Medical Research have worked tirelessly to convince Congress and President Bush to ease the restrictions. *Newsweek*'s issue of October 25, 2004, quotes Republican senator Orrin Hatch of Utah: "There is no greater way to promote life than to find a way to defeat death and disease. Stem-cell research may provide a way to do that." This issue is likely to continue generating strong emotions for years to come, and religious beliefs will play an important role on both sides of the ongoing discussion.

It is easy to see how religious beliefs play into debates like those surrounding stem-cell research. However, these are by no means the only issues in which voters' and elected officials' religious beliefs are affecting political policy. Today, the newest battle on the front lines between religion and politics is the issue of same-sex marriage.

# Chapter 6

RELIGION & MODERN CULTURE

## SAME-SEX MARRIAGE

On May 17, 2004, Massachusetts became the first U.S. state to allow same-sex marriage. According to CBSNEWS.com, more than one thousand same-sex couples applied for a marriage license that very day. On Boston's Beacon Hill, a **Unitarian Universalist** minister married one of those couples, Julie and Hillary Goodridge. People gathered for the ceremony cheered and threw rainbow confetti.

Marriage

Three years earlier, a Boston City clerk had rejected Julie and Hillary's first marriage license application. Julie and Hillary were among seven couples who filed a lawsuit in November of 2003. This suit prompted the Massachusetts' Supreme Judicial Court to rule in favor of same-sex marriage. But the coast is not totally clear yet for same-sex marriages in Massachusetts. In 2006, voters will be able to decide whether to alter their state constitution to ban same-sex marriages and define them as civil unions. This possible change in status has many people on edge.

There are several political positions regarding same-sex marriage. One is to support such marriages with all the same rights and privileges as heterosexual marriage. Another position would allow same-sex civil unions, legal arrangements that grant privileges similar to those given by marriage, but not precisely the same as marriage. A third position is opposition to both civil unions and same-sex marriage.

An ABC News poll taken in January 2004 found: "Most Americans agree with President Bush's opposition to same-sex marriage—but most also oppose amending the U.S. Constitution to ban it, saying instead that it should be a matter for the individual states to decide." The survey found "38 percent of Americans favor amending the U.S. Constitution to make it illegal for homosexual couples to marry, but 58 percent say, instead, that each state should make its own laws on gay marriage." Furthermore, a majority of Americans—55 percent—believe same-sex marriage should not become legal.

The question of same-sex marriage is the new hot political issue in the United States. In the 2004 elections, eleven states—Arkansas, Georgia, Kentucky, Michigan, Mississippi, Montana, North Dakota, Ohio, Oklahoma, Oregon, and Utah—proposed amending their state constitutions to ban same-sex marriages. The proposals passed in all eleven states. In eight of the states, the ban was also on all civil unions (including those between heterosexual couples). Some political commentators have suggested having the issue of same-sex marriage on the ballot may even have swayed the 2004 election in favor of George W.

# GLOSSARY

**celibate**: The state of abstaining from sexual intercourse and marriage.

**chastity**: Abstinance from sexual intercourse.

**Conservative Judaism**: A branch of Judaism that follows the Torah and the Talmud, but not as strictly as Orthodox Judaism, making allowances for changing times and circumstances.

**ghostwriter**: An author who writes under someone else's name. Famous people often hire ghostwriters who do their actual writing, while the books are published under the more well-known name.

**inextricably**: Unable to escape or be separated from something.

**inherently**: Part of the nature of something; part of something's essential character.

**lobby**: To influence or sway a political official in a desired direction.

**Orthodox Judaism**: A branch of Judaism that strictly follows the Torah and Talmud in their daily lives.

**Reform Judaism**: A branch of Judaism marked by the nonobservance of much legal tradition considered irrelevant in the present and the shortening and simplification of traditional rituals.

**Unitarian Universalist**: A member of a religious group that defines itself as "a liberal religion that promotes acceptance of one another, encourages spiritual growth in our congregations and affirms a free and responsible search for truth and meaning."

## MARRIAGE? CIVIL UNION?
## WHAT'S THE DIFFERENCE?

Marriages and civil unions are commitments between two individuals. The difference between marriages and civil unions has much to do with who recognizes the commitment. Marriage establishes kinship between two people, making them spouses. Civil marriages are performed by a civil authority like a judge. Religious marriages are performed by a religious authority such as a priest or rabbi. Most governments recognize both civil and religious marriages as legitimate legal commitments, regardless of the religion or legal jurisdiction in which the marriage took place.

Many governments, however, define marriage as a legal union between a man and a woman, which means commitments between same-sex couples cannot be legally recognized. Some have proposed the term "civil unions" be applied to such commitments. Currently in the United States, civil unions exist only in Vermont, which began recognizing civil unions in 2000 and Connecticut, where the Civil Union Law was passed in 2005. Although civil unions have some of the same rights and responsibilities associated with civil and religious marriages, they are not recognized as legal relationships outside the state.

*"I haven't changed in the sense that I believe sexuality is a gift from God to be expressed exclusively within the commitment of heterosexual marriage. . . . However, I do not believe that gives you a license to hate people. . . . I have sat and listened to story after story after story from gay people of their journey and have cried with them and tried to listen to the awful pain they go through. . . . 'Whom you would change you must first love.' Martin Luther King, Jr. said that."*

—Ed Dobson, *former vice president of Moral Majority*

Bush. Ohio was the final, crucial factor giving Bush the electoral-college votes he needed to win. The proposal on the Ohio ballot to ban same-sex marriage may have motivated more politically conservative voters to get to the polls in that state.

## RELIGIOUS BELIEFS & SAME-SEX MARRIAGE

Religion plays a definite role in the same-sex marriage issue. Christians hold diverse views regarding homosexuality, what the Bible says about homosexuality, and what place gays and lesbians should hold in churches and society. Historically, many religions in North America have opposed the practice of homosexuality. More recently, some Protestant churches, some branches of Judaism, and a growing number of gay and lesbian church groups have worked to foster greater public acceptance of homosexuals. Even among religious groups that believe homosexuality is sinful, a number of believers support laws that would ensure gays and lesbians have the same legal rights as all other citizens.

A number of conservative religious groups, including the Christian Coalition, Traditional Values Coalition, Focus on the Family, and the Eagle Forum, oppose same-sex marriage. Some of these groups **lobby** at state and federal levels, have great access to the media, and use their influence by speaking for or against certain politicians. In his book *Homosexuality and the Politics of Truth,* Jeffrey Satinover represents their perspective: "In the end the debate over homosexual behavior and . . . public policy can only be concluded . . . on moral grounds, and moral grounds will ultimately mean religious grounds." Satinover and many other evangelicals establish their opinions on homosexuality from literal interpretations of specific biblical passages, particularly Leviticus 20:13: "If a man lies with a male as with a woman, both of them have committed an abomination; they shall be put to death; their blood is upon them," and Romans 1:26–27:

For this reason God gave them up to degrading passions. Their women exchange natural intercourse for unnatural, and in the same way also the men, giving up natural intercourse with women, were consumed with passion for one another. Men committed shameless acts with men and received in their own persons the due penalty for their error.

The Roman Catholic Church has stated

men and women with homosexual tendencies must be accepted with respect, compassion and sensitivity. Every sign of unjust discrimination in their regard should be avoided." However, the Church opposes same-sex marriage, believing that instead of entering into life-long partnerships, homosexuals "are called . . . to live the virtue of **chastity**.

## A SHOW OF ACCEPTANCE

The United Church of Christ (UCC) denomination encourages participation of gays and lesbians in their churches and supports their
equal rights in the larger society. In December 2004, CBS and NBC
refused to air a commercial produced by the UCC that highlighted
the church's welcome of gays and lesbians. The ads featured two
muscle-bound bouncers standing outside a church, selecting people
who could attend services and those who could not. Among those
kept out was a homosexual couple. The ad declared, "Jesus didn't
turn people away, neither do we."

Southern Baptists teach that homosexuality is a sin, that homosexuals can change if they desire, and that homosexuals must remain
*celibate*. They have passed numerous resolutions condemning homosexuality, including a 1998 resolution opposing any attempt by the government to provide "endorsement, sanction, recognition, acceptance or
civil rights advantage on the basis of homosexuality."

An increasing number of gays and lesbians in North America say
there is no conflict between their sexual orientation and Christian faith.
They point out that although certain passages of the Bible may con-
demn homosexual behavior, the Bible also contains numerous prohibi-
tions that most people believe no longer apply. They argue that unwa-
veringly literal interpretations of the Bible can cause people to lose sight
of its larger message of love and acceptance.

RELIGION & MODERN CULTURE

Civil Rights

*"The Bible contains six admonishments to homo-sexuals and 362 admonishments to heterosexuals. That doesn't mean that God doesn't love hetero-sexuals. It's just that they need more supervision."*
—Lynn Lavner, *entertainer*

Mel White was once a **ghostwriter** for Billy Graham, Jerry Falwell, and Pat Robertson before he admitted his homosexuality. White now says, "Jesus makes it perfectly clear. God is not waiting in the padded pews of mega-churches that turn lesbians and gays into outcasts. God is out there in the world struggling to relieve the suffering of all Her oppressed and forgotten children."

The Universal Fellowship of Metropolitan Community Churches (MCC) is a Christian denomination composed largely of gays, lesbians, and their supporters. Thirty years ago, Troy Perry, a Pentecostal preacher, admitted he was gay. His church fired him and his family left him. Lacking a church to go to as a gay man, he began his own church. Today, Perry's MCC has 314 congregations in sixteen countries, making it the world's largest religious denomination for gays and lesbians. Each year, MCC ministers preside over five thousand "holy union" ceremonies for same-sex couples.

The existence of gay and lesbian churches and denominations does not signal broad acceptance of homosexuality in conservative Christian circles. A 2001 survey by the Barna group found that among people who consider themselves "born-again Christians," 27 percent said "gay and lesbian lifestyles are morally acceptable," while 66 percent said they were "unacceptable." In the same survey, 95 percent of those who consider themselves "Evangelical or fundamentalist" were of the opinion that "gay and lesbian lifestyles are morally unacceptable."

Some conservative Christians, despite being personally morally opposed to homosexuality, still defend the rights of gays and lesbians. The issue for these Christians is the protection of civil rights for all citizens. They feel antidiscrimination laws, civil union rights, and other legal protections for gays and lesbians are part of Jesus's command to love all people unconditionally. These people of faith support equal rights for same-sex couples because they see the issue as a matter of love, justice, basic fairness, and civil rights. However, very few want to see the term "marriage" used for both heterosexual and homosexual unions. Many with these beliefs advocate civil unions, which would provide same-sex couples with the same rights and privileges afforded to married couples, but want to see the term "marriage" reserved specifically for heterosexual unions. For many people, this appears to be a compromise that would give everyone what they want, allowing same-sex couples to have legally recognized unions and allowing the term "marriage" to be retained for specifically heterosexual unions. However, other people see such distinctions as *inherently* unequal. They compare such a compromise to segregation and the concept of "separate but equal," an idea that the civil rights movement ultimately showed was unacceptable.

Judaism varies in its approach to homosexuality. **Reform Judaism** is fully accepting of practicing gays and lesbians. **Orthodox Judaism** requires gays and lesbians to remain celibate. **Conservative Judaism**, like many Christian denominations, is struggling with the issue. They will not perform same-sex weddings, and each local rabbi is free to choose whether he or she will allow participation in synagogue life for gays and lesbians.

## CURRENT POLITICAL STATUS OF SAME-SEX MARRIAGE IN THE UNITED STATES & CANADA

President George W. Bush pushed for Congress to amend the U.S. Constitution to outlaw same-sex marriage during the 2004 legislative session. The nonbinding resolution cleared the House of Representatives, but the Senate blocked it. Karl Rove, Bush's top strategist, has

## A COMMON MISCONCEPTION

While many religious groups and individuals oppose same-sex marriage based on biblical teachings, others oppose same-sex marriage because they believe that, if legalized, it would force religious institutions into marrying same-sex couples. This, however, is a misconception. Not all marriages are religious marriages. Many are secular, performed by civil authorities such as judges, magistrates, or justices of the peace. Although a legalization of same-sex marriage would require that states grant marriage licenses and that civil authorities perform marriages for same-sex couples, it could not force religious institutions into granting religious marriages to these couples. For example, a Catholic church cannot be required to marry a Muslim couple (or a couple of any other religion). Similarly, the state cannot require that private religious organizations marry same-sex couples.

*"For many Canadians and many Parliamentarians, this is a difficult issue involving personal and religious convictions and it represents a very significant change to a long-standing institution."*
—Canadian Prime Minister Paul Martin

said that the president is committed to pushing for a constitutional amendment to ban gay marriage during his second term.

In Canada at present, six provinces and one territory issue marriage licenses to same-sex couples. Canada's federal government currently defines marriage as "between one man and one woman." In 2003, however, the Ontario Court of Appeals ruled that such a definition violated the Canadian Charter of Rights and Freedoms. The court's ruling required Ontario to begin immediately issuing marriage licenses to same-sex couples, and other provinces and territories have followed suit. The federal government is expected to change the official definition of marriage in 2005. In December 2004, Canada's Supreme Court also weighed in on the issue by offering a nonbinding opinion supporting both the parliament's ability to redefine marriage and religious leaders' rights to refuse to perform same-sex marriage ceremonies. Commenting on his intention to introduce legislation that will change the definition of marriage, Canadian prime minister Paul Martin said, "For many Canadians and many Parliamentarians, this is a difficult issue involving personal and religious convictions and it represents a very significant change to a long-standing institution."

After the Supreme Court's opinion was handed down, the *Washington Post* commented, "The court opinion was the latest sign that Canada is on a different track from its southern neighbor, where referendums banning gay marriage passed in 11 states last month." Douglas Elliott, a

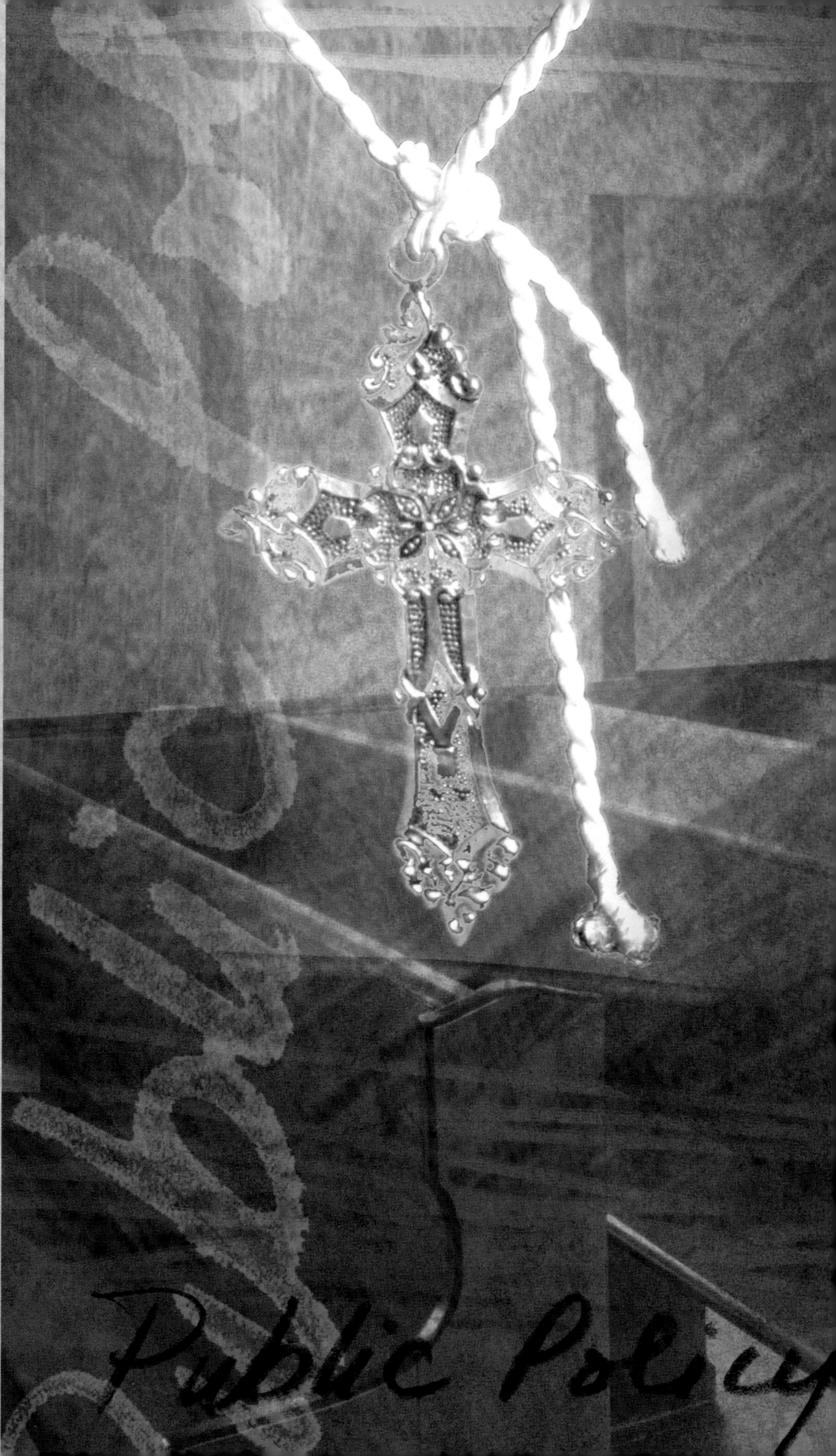
Public Policy

Toronto lawyer involved in the Supreme Court case and president of an international association that monitors laws affecting homosexuals commented, "Canada is without a doubt one of the best—if not the best—places to live as a gay or lesbian person. It's hard to believe that just a river separates us from the reality in the United States."

Issues like abortion, stem-cell research, and same-sex marriage are without a doubt the most openly religiously charged issues in North American politics today. For many voters and elected officials, it is almost impossible to separate their personal religious beliefs on issues like these from their beliefs about public policy on these issues. However, these controversial topics are by no means the only politically relevant issues influenced by religious and moral viewpoints. For many people, religion and morality are *inextricably* woven into how they view the world and approach life. Attitudes toward protection of the environment, alleviation of poverty, and social activism are also often tied to a moral or religious sense of obligation and duty to the world and to humankind.

# Chapter 7

# THE ENVIRONMENT, POVERTY, & SOCIAL ACTIVISM

The Ojibwa/Chippewa Nation call them-selves Anishinabe, meaning "The People." At one time, they controlled more territory than any other Native tribe in North America. Their land stretched from what are today the states of Michigan, Wiscon-sin, Minnesota, and North Dakota to the Canadian provinces of Ontario, Manitoba, and Saskatchewan. Like all Native people, the Ojibwa relied on the land for their very existence. With the coming of the Euro-peans, their lives drastically changed. By the end of the twentieth century, the United States and Canada had taken possession of most of their land through treaties and land **cessions**. The result was an impoverished Ojibwa people.

betting Active

*"Only when the last tree is cut; only when the last river is polluted; only when the last fish is caught; only then will they realize that you cannot eat money."*

—*Cree Indian Proverb*

Over the years, Native people have risen up to help their tribes win back some of their lands. Winona LaDuke, for example, a Mississippi Band, White Earth Anishinabe of the Bear Clan born in 1959, became active in American Indian environmental issues while attending Harvard University. Since graduating, she has become a major voice for American Indian environmental and political rights. LaDuke settled on the White Earth reservation and joined Anishinabe Akeeng, a land rights organization at the Ojibwa reservation.

The group strives to get back some of the lands that were taken from them by federal, state, and county governments. They are motivated by traditional spiritual beliefs that state humans are required to care for the environment. Anishinabe Akeeng is concerned about the physical and spiritual dimensions of the land, water, air, and all natural resources. It has organized protests and marches and initiated legal efforts to reclaim Anishinabe land.

When legal options ran out, LaDuke started the White Earth Land Recovery Project (WELP). This group hopes to reacquire enough land to support traditional farmers and craftspeople, and they hope to grow plants and herbs to provide traditional medicines.

## CHRISTIAN CONCERN FOR THE ENVIRONMENT

By their example, *indigenous* people who practice traditional ways have encouraged many Christians to think more about their responsibility to the environment. While Christians do not regard the earth as their mother in the same way that Native religions do, they do regard it as a valuable gift from the Creator. The Bible, similar to some Native traditions, says God formed human beings from the earth.

Some Christians who hold to a particular view of *end-time prophecies* feel they have little obligation to care for the environment. Believing that the end of the world will come soon, they are not concerned with preserving it. A few have even interpreted looming ecological catastrophes as a signal that Christ will soon return.

An increasing number of Christians, however, share a growing sense of ecological concern. They see Genesis chapter 1 as God's charge to protect and care for creation. They also read of God's love for the natural world throughout the Psalms and other books of the Bible. These Christians believe that concern for the environment is connected with issues of health and justice for fellow human beings.

## CRISIS IN AFRICA

Seventy-five percent of the forty-two million people in the world who live with HIV live in sub-Saharan Africa. Every day, 6,500 Africans die of AIDS. Approximately 2.5 million Africans are expected to die in 2005 because they lack the medicine needed to fight the illness.

## BONO SPEAKS OUT FOR AIDS VICTIMS

Religious and spiritual beliefs do not only lead people to feel a responsibility toward the Earth; they also lead them to feel a responsibility toward their fellow human beings. Most of us can do small things in our own lives—like volunteering with a community organization, visiting someone who is sick, financially supporting a humanitarian aid effort, or just listening to someone who needs to talk—that help to make the world a better place. People who have achieved great financial success or public recognition often have the opportunity to make an even more far-reaching impact. Some people who achieve fame and fortune are motivated by their religious or spiritual ideals to use that fame and fortune for a greater good. Bono, the lead singer from the rock group U2, is one such example. He spends time, energy, and money knocking on political

*"Well, you know, I am not a very good advertisement for God, so I generally don't wear that badge on my lapel. But it is certainly written on the inside. I am a believer. There are 2,103 verses of Scripture pertaining to the poor. Jesus Christ only speaks of judgment once. . . . It is about the poor. 'I was naked and you clothed me. I was a stranger and you let me in.' This is at the heart of the gospel."*

—Bono, quoted in the United Methodist News Report Online

doors for the poor and for an issue that he sees as the globe's largest emergency, the AIDS epidemic in Africa.

One of Bono's major tactics for addressing the AIDS crisis has been testifying before the U.S. Congress, trying to convince Congress to cancel the debts owed by the world's poorest nations. If African nations did not have to make constant debt payments, they would be able to spend more of their limited funds on the AIDS epidemic. As it stands, they spend around $13.5 billion a year repaying debts to rich countries—and less than half that amount on health care. Bono is also hoping that pharmaceutical companies will give free HIV drugs to African patients.

Bono's Jubilee 2000 campaign was his largest social campaign. He took along supporters such as Radiohead's Thom Yorke, Live Aid organizer Bob Geldof, and music producer Quincy Jones. Bono spoke before the United Nations and the U.S. Congress and met with some important people such as Bill Clinton and Pope John Paul II.

But not everyone understands or agrees with Bono's movement. In an appearance on *Oprah*, there was a question-and-answer session with

Bono. A woman stood up and praised Bono for his efforts to alleviate AIDS, but she went on to say that for many Americans there are poverty issues in their own backyards that need attention—shouldn't they be taking care of those? Bono graciously agreed that there are real needs in all communities. However, he also said that America doesn't experience more than six thousand people dying each day, like people do in Africa. Bono likened the African emergency to a historical example. He asked, if China had had the cure for the bubonic plague in Europe that wiped out one-third of the world's population and didn't give it to those in Europe, what opinion would the world have had of China? There is no cure for AIDS, but Bono believes that America has the treatments necessary to end the AIDS crisis in Africa; he questions how the world will look at the United States if it does nothing.

In November 2000, Bono began to see results. Congress passed legislation giving $435 million in debt relief to poor countries.

## RELIGIOUS BELIEFS & PROTESTS AGAINST INJUSTICE

The sun shimmers off the Nevada desert sand on a warm summer day in 1990. A chain-link fence cuts across the barren countryside. Large, bright signs warn, "US Government test site—trespassing strictly prohibited." Military police patrol the perimeter in jeeps and on foot. Outside the fence, a convoy of vehicles pulls up. Several dozen people get out of the cars. They walk together to a space just outside the fence and then gather in a circle. They read from the Bible and sing spiritual songs. Then, one by one, men and women leave the circle and head for the fence. Two members have removed links so others can crawl under the fence. As they enter the forbidden test site, some run, some literally dance, and others walk resolutely toward the zone where researchers will soon detonate weapons of mass destruction.

## MENNONITE CHURCH CANADA
## SPREADING HOPE AROUND THE WORLD

A young South African woman named Zolisa strokes the head of her two-year-old son. She knows she won't have much more time to be with him. Like one out of five South Africans, Zolisa has been infected with HIV. Her case is very advanced. She cannot care for herself, but tells a pastor, "I met Mama Mawela. She is helping me. I am powerless and she brings me food boosters and medicines." Mama Mawela is one of many volunteers trained by the Transkei AIDS Support Organization (TRASO) and now working in their local communities. TRASO is supported financially and with volunteers from the Mennonite Church Canada.

For more than a century, Mennonites in Canada have been actively involved in promoting peace and justice. They regularly provide both financial and volunteer services to address poverty, disaster relief, hunger, and other human needs throughout the world.

This is the Nevada nuclear test site. From 1951 to 1958, the U.S. government exploded nuclear bombs aboveground, exposing thousands of ranchers to radioactive fallout. Recently, the government has paid some of them for the suffering they experienced from cancer caused by the tests. From 1961 to 1992, the government exploded nuclear weapons underground. The government claims these tests were harm-

## THE BOMB-BREAKING BERRIGANS

During the 1960s, Phillip and Daniel Berrigan, brothers and Catholic priests, became famous for pouring human blood on draft files and burning draft records to protest the Vietnam War. Philip spent eleven years and Daniel spent four years in prison as a consequence of their actions. In his autobiography, *To Dwell in Peace*, Daniel says their tactics were, "ways we inherited from Gandhi and King and above all, from Jesus."

After the Vietnam War, Philip and Daniel protested against nuclear weapons. They began the Plowshares Movement (from Isaiah, "beat swords into plowshares"), which involved destruction of government war-making apparatus. Some of their tactics included hammering nuclear warheads and splashing blood on classified documents. Philip Berrigan wrote: "Our critics say that attacking atomic weapons with ball peen hammers is an act of violence. Destroying property, they insist, is a form of violence. At best, it is a curious argument, one I've heard many times before. Warheads whose sole purpose is to vaporize cities are hardly to be thought legitimate property. Bombs that indiscriminately murder millions of men, women and children are not 'property.'"

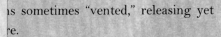

...s sometimes "vented," releasing yet
...re.

...d early 1990s, protesters would fre-
...nuclear test site. Sometimes these ac-
...Military police would handcuff tres-
...aking federal law.

... of civil disobedience, the deliberate
...willingness to accept the consequences
...ng a fine or going to jail) as a form of
...onstrate the injustice of the law being
broken.

For thousands of years, religious beliefs have prompted some people to perform costly actions of civil disobedience. In the words of the first Christians, "We must obey the laws of God rather than man." In the 1960s, civil disobedience tactics were important for blacks, Hispanics, and American Indians seeking equal rights. At the same time, activists used civil disobedience to protest the Vietnam War.

For many protesters, religion was an important reason for civil disobedience. Dr. Martin Luther King Jr. believed that civil disobedience was much more than a means to political ends. It was a way to live that influenced a person's daily life and deeds. The guidelines of the SCLC stated, "Remember always that the nonviolent movement seeks justice and reconciliation—not victory." For Dr. King and many others, nonviolence was a sign of agape, the unconditional love that God has for every human being.

Politically conservative, as well as liberal protesters, have used civil disobedience. During the 1980s, Operation Rescue volunteers would chain themselves to abortion clinic doors and form human "chains" blocking entrances. They did so believing they were saving unborn human lives. Many paid enormous fines and spent months in jail. They believed fines and jail were a small price to pay for saving a life.

Civil disobedience is the most radical—and most costly—form of political involvement. Few U.S. citizens engage in such actions. At the

Peace.

> *"Peace activist A. J. Muste said, 'There is no way to peace, peace is the way.' He meant that we realize peace right in the present moment with each look, smile, word and action. Peace is not just an end. Each step we make should be peace, should be joy, should be happiness."*
>
> —*Buddhist teacher Thich Nhat Hanh*, Living Buddha, Living Christ

same time, civil disobedience is part of a much larger picture. Millions of Americans express their religious beliefs by taking part in political activities. They may vote or they may take part in political campaigns. They might attend rallies or carry signs in protests. Some hand out leaflets; others make phone calls attempting to convince other citizens of their beliefs.

The separation of church and state continues to be an ideal that many U.S. and Canadian citizens hold dear. Even so, whether intentional or unintentional, religion and politics continue to mix in significant and sometimes unexpected ways. They have done so for centuries and continue to do so. Timid and aggressive, conservative and liberal, Buddhist and Christian, North American citizens speak, live, and often vote their spiritual beliefs.

Furthermore, the separation of church and state is clearly an ideal that not everyone in North America believes in. Though they may differ in many ways, religious citizens who believe religion should play a role in political policy are convinced a higher law stands above all human government. The human-created obligation that state and church be separate will do little to convince them otherwise.

Balmer, Randall. *Religion in Twentieth Century America*. New York: Oxford University Press, 2001.

Flanders, Carl N. *Library in a Book: Abortion*. New York: Facts On File, 1991.

Gay, Kathlyn. *Church and State: Government and Religion in the United States*. Brookfield, Conn.: Millbrook Press, 1992.

Gonzales, Doreen. *Cesar Chavez: Leader for Migrant Farm Workers*. Brooklyn Heights, N.J.: Enslow, 1996.

Herda, D. J. *Roe v. Wade: The Abortion Question*. Hillside, N.J.: Enslow, 1994.

McIntosh, Kenneth. *Born Again Believers: Evangelicals and Charismatics*. Philadelphia, Pa.: Mason Crest, 2005.

Sider, Ron. *Just Generosity: A New Vision for Overcoming Poverty in America*. Grand Rapids, Mich.: Baker Books, 1999.

Stockman, Steve. *Walk On: The Spiritual Journey of U2*. Orlando, Fla.: Relevant Books, 2001.

Viegas, Jennifer. *Stem Cell Research*. New York: Rosen, 2003.

Wald, Kenneth D. *Religion and Politics in the United States*, 3rd ed. Washington, D.C.: Congressional Quarterly Press, 1997.

# FOR MORE INFORMATION

Bill of Rights
www.law.cornell.edu/constitution
/constitution.billofrights.html

Bread for the World
www.bread.org

Christian Coalition of America
www.cc.org

Crisis Pregnancy Centers
www.pregnancycenters.org

Crossing Over Ministry (formerly
Roe no More Ministry)
www.roenomore.org

First Amendment Center
www.firstamendmentcenter.org

Focus on the Family with Dr.
James Dobson: www.family.org

Gay Rights: Overview
www.publicagenda.org

Jerry Falwell Ministries
www.falwell.com

Pew Forum
www.pewforum.org/religion-
politics

Rainbow/PUSH Coalition
www.rainbowpush.org

Religious Tolerance
www.religioustolerance.org

The One Campaign
www.theonecampaign.org

Publisher's note:
The Web sites listed on this page were active at the time of publication.
The publisher is not responsible for Web sites that have changed their
addresses or discontinued operation since the date of publication. The
publisher will review and update the Web-site list upon each reprint.

# PICTURE CREDITS

The illustrations in RELIGION AND MODERN CULTURE are photo montages made by Dianne Hodack. They are a combination of her original mixed-media paintings and collages, the photography of Benjamin Stewart, various historical public-domain artwork, and other royalty-free photography collections.

AUTHORS: Kenneth and Marsha McIntosh are former teachers. They have two children, Jonathan, nineteen, and Eirené, sixteen. Marsha has a bachelor's of science degree in Bible and education, and Kenneth has a bachelor's degree in English education and a master's degree in theology. They live in Flagstaff, Arizona, with their children, a dog, and two cats. Kenneth frequently speaks on topics of religion and society. Kenneth and Marsha have been involved in a variety of political causes over the past two decades.

CONSULTANT: Dr. Marcus J. Borg is the Hundere Distinguished Professor of Religion and Culture in the Philosophy Department at Oregon State University. Dr. Borg is past president of the Anglican Association of Biblical Scholars. Internationally known as a biblical and Jesus scholar, the *New York Times* called him "a leading figure among this generation of Jesus scholars." He is the author of twelve books, which have been translated into eight languages. Among them are *The Heart of Christianity: Rediscovering a Life of Faith* (2003) and *Meeting Jesus Again for the First Time* (1994), the best-selling book by a contemporary Jesus scholar.

CONSULTANT: Dr. Robert K. Johnston is Professor of Theology and Culture at Fuller Theological Seminary in Pasadena, California, having served previously as Provost of North Park University and as a faculty member of Western Kentucky University. The author or editor of thirteen books and twenty-five book chapters (including *The Christian at Play*, 1983; *The Variety of American Evangelicalism*, 1991; *Reel Spirituality: Theology and Film in Dialogue*, 2000; *Life Is Not Work/Work Is Not Life: Simple Reminders for Finding Balance in a 24/7 World*, 2000; *Finding God in the Movies: 33 Films of Reel Faith*, 2004; and *Useless Beauty: Ecclesiastes Through the Lens of Contemporary Film*, 2004), Johnston is the immediate past president of the American Theological Society, an ordained Protestant minister, and an avid bodysurfer.